SUMMER OF SPORT

Nargis Lal

MINERVA PRESS
MONTREUX   LONDON   WASHINGTON

SUMMER OF SPORT
Copyright © Nargis Lal 1995

All Rights Reserved

ISBN 1 85863 569 1

First Published 1995 by
MINERVA PRESS
1 Cromwell Place
London SW7 2JE

Printed in Great Britain by
B.W.D. Ltd., Northolt, Middlesex.

SUMMER OF SPORT

1

EDINBURGH 1970

"England have got a Paki girl in their team. What a sham." The Glasgow youth slurped down his beer. He pawed the list for the Edinburgh Commonwealth Games and swore his indignation. The barman disapproved and rolled his eyes at the staff.

"I want this lot out of here," he murmured.

"At least we don't have one," said a friend of the youth.

"What's a nigger doing on an English team?"

"Better hope it's the first and last time," said another. "We don't want 'em representing Britain." He straightened his shoulders at the thought. White Scotland must be ready for battle.

The girl they spoke of was not far from their hotel bar. She was sharing salad in a restaurant with another white Scot: her former boyfriend and a hero of the hotel boys. She was Rehana Hassan, born in England and running for her country in her first Commonwealth Games. He was Andrew Raymond, the Rangers mid-fielder and her lover during his 1969 spell with London's West Ham. They had parted good friends when he came home. Britain did not yet know the girl he knew so well. Before long, the nation would know almost every detail of her life.

2

The essence of Muslim belief is this: there is no God but God (Allah) and Muhammed is His messenger. Muslims can be black, brown or white and can be born in any country in the world. Some are born into the faith; others convert. Some are known as Shi'ites; others as Sunnis. Roughly speaking, the Shi'ites believe in martyrdom. They beat and pound at their brains until their heads are bloody. The Sunnis make up most of the Muslim community in Britain. Many of their forebears were born in the vast sub-continent of South Asia, at a time when it was just known as India. In August 1947, as India won independence from the British Empire, a large part of its Muslim community heralded the birth of Pakistan. Much later, a new state called Bangladesh was founded in East Pakistan.

In early 1947, Aftar Tahira Azaruddin left Karachi, in the Muslim north west of India, to join her lecturer husband in the faraway country of England. Married for just six months, and newly pregnant, she packed her prayer books and her university degree and boarded the ship with Yusuf al-Haq, a family friend and her chaperone. They docked in Egypt, a Muslim land, and Aftar wept at thoughts of her family at home. Outside the pyramids she began to feel weak, and suddenly threw up the Cairo curry. Finally, exhausted by seasickness and anxiety, she stepped on to the shores of the colonial power and prayed in Arabic for her future child to find success in a foreign land.

NOVEMBER 1963

Zakir Hassan was a stoic man. Most of the time he loved his wife and daughters and his lectureship at London University, but tonight his wife kept exploding.

"She's gone running again! No time for her homework." And she spilled ghee on to her pale pink sari, which made her madder. "It's all your fault. You encourage her."

He considered that accusation as he watched their elder child sprint away.

"We have to let her do it, Aftar," he said calmly. "Remember what her teacher said. Our daughter could be national junior champion."

"Could be. What about her studies? What if she doesn't succeed? She must have qualifications behind her."

Dr Hassan shook his head.

"She'll get her exams. She's got a brain. We have to encourage her talent." He eased some coal into the fire. "In this freezing cold she still goes to that track. This is not just a game for her."

"Well, I suppose I'm just too much of an academic to understand."

"Aftar, I'm an academic too! Have you forgotten we teach in the same university?"

Her mood lightened, as it always did after a tantrum. She laughed, and they turned their thoughts to dinner - to chapatis and korma - and the killing of John F. Kennedy. From upstairs came the strains of Lennon and McCartney.

"What can we do?" Zakir shrugged. "One daughter runs all the time, the other wants to marry Paul McCartney."

"You know, she's no fool. I wanted to marry Ashok Kumar."

"And instead of a great movie star you ended up with an old language teacher."

"Old and sports mad! Go and call Sana for dinner."

Sana, on the verge of her teens, piled salad on to her plate and complained that her sister was out again.

"Rehana's always out," she sulked. "I want her to help me with my hair."

"With your hair?" Zakir chuckled. "I think Rehana has better things to do."

"What time will she be back?" Sana persisted.

"She'll be gone at least another hour yet," Aftar said. "She'll be hungry, I've left a plate for her."

"Can't I have her chapati?"

"No. Now eat."

Later, they heard their daughter's key in the door and went to meet her.

"Mr Lewis is here," Rehana said. Bob Lewis, her school sports teacher and club coach, nodded from the garden path. The Finchley streets were quiet. North London was getting some snow and a gelid wind blew inside.

"Come in," Zakir urged. "Tell us how she's getting on."

Bob sat down in the comfortable front room. They offered him tea and he remembered Muslims did not drink alcohol.

Mr Lewis was a little in awe of Rehana's parents. What he saw around him magnified his shame; he wished he knew as much about Shakespeare and Keats as these immigrants did. He looked at the Eastern art on the walls, at the Holy Qu'ran resting with pride on a carved mahogany base. Staring at him were books in Arabic and French, and the full set of the Encyclopaedia Britannica. On a glass coffee table sat 'The Times' and, to his great relief, a magazine about more frivolous things - movie stars in India. He clasped the cup of tea and tried to relax in his seat.

"Rehana is running so well," he said, "that I don't think I can keep up with her." He saw pride in Zakir's face, uncertainty in Aftar's. "I've been running the club for two years. I have to move back to Cardiff next autumn and I'm looking for someone with a lot of coaching experience to take Rehana on. First, I want to enter her in a national schools' contest, if you agree."

"Doesn't she need to qualify first?" Aftar asked. She was trying to stall.

"Mrs Hassan, Rehana's 800 metre runs are so good for a sixteen year old that she's already qualified ten times over. She'll be running for England before we know it."

"For England?" Aftar repeated. "I never dreamed she was so good."

Bob smiled. "Rehana says you were an excellent athlete back in Karachi."

"A long time ago. I used to run at school, but I never thought about it when I left. Can she have inherited that?"

"It looks as though she has."

1964

Spring came. Sana had become a teenager and wanted to march in Memphis with Martin Luther King. Rehana helped her write letters against segregation but did not see very much of her. She ran every day after school and won the 800 metres at the English Schools Championship with ease.

"Your daughter is a future star," the Hassans' friends told them, but Aftar worried about Rehana running for England.

"England is not ready for that," she said to her husband. "We made a mistake having our children in this country. Everywhere they go they get called Blackie, even in school. If only she could run for Pakistan."

"Our girls are Westernised," Zakir said. "It's too late."

On a wet Sunday in June, the Hassans were invited to Birmingham for lunch with friends. Rehana had to stay in London for a gruelling practice run she really wanted to avoid. Sana did not want to go.

"I want to stay at home," she moaned. "Why can't I?"

"Because Vijay and Prema are very close friends," Aftar said. "They'll be expecting at least one of our children. Look, you can bring your Beatles tape for the car. Hurry up."

"Okay. Rehana gets to do whatever she wants!"

"Rehana doesn't want to run today," Zakir interjected. "We'd better leave, we have to be there by one."

Rehana pulled on her running shoes and flew upstairs for the rest of her kit.

"See you later tonight," her parents called. "Khudafiz."

Thereafter, Rehana's family ceased to exist. A fatal crash on the motorway back from Birmingham wiped them out. Bob Lewis had driven his student home and found two cars in the drive blocking his way. Tom Myers from the university came towards them, with two of the Hassans' friends. At first Tom Myers only said there had been an accident, and Rehana's stomach began to ache. Her Aunt Lakshmi guided her to a chair and began to cry as she told her that her parents and Sana were dead.

Islam buries people within hours of their death. Therefore there was no time for anyone to come from Pakistan, and there were no blood relatives at the funerals. Always independent, even as a child, Rehana turned down her aunts' and uncles' requests for her to live in Karachi. She could not live in another country, away from her running, and there was another thing - she had never been to Pakistan and was afraid of the traditions that she and Sana had escaped. She stayed in Finchley with her parents' friends, but grieved alone. Everyone noticed that she was unable to cry. She would not talk about the deaths and Bob said she had not really registered her loss. As the summer term ended Rehana left school. Her parents would have wanted her to go to university, but she wanted to spend her energy on training. She found a local office job with a firm that packed frozen foods. With her parents' house sold she moved into a tiny flat near the club, a rare step for a single Asian girl. The Tokyo Olympic Games more or less passed her by. She was not in a mood to concentrate, but she was thrilled to see Britain's Ann Packer win the 800 metres gold and dreamed she might one day do the same. Though she did not know it, she was still in shock. She was running to keep her mind off the pain.

"How much do you know about Denmark?" Bob asked her. She had knocked a fraction of a second off her 800 metres speed and was relaxing with a Coke.

"Denmark. Uh, not much. They eat a lot of bacon."

Bob laughed. "Well, that's true. But they also have some good runners and I've been talking to one of their ex-champions. His name's Peter Andersen." He sat down. "Rehana, I've asked him to take over the club. He's a very experienced coach and that's what you need. He's coming here tomorrow."

"So you're really going."

Was she ready to face losing someone else?

"Don't worry. You're going to hit it off just great with him."

Peter Andersen was forty five. He had silver grey hair and an almost permanent look of solemnity. He was a former European champion, in London for a new life with his English girlfriend. He came to the club to watch the young athletes. His attention focused on the slight seventeen year old running around the faded track. Bob came up next to him and said, "I don't have the push to get the best out of her. You have."

Peter watched her run over the next few days. He took over the club and spoke to its star. His words stunned her.

"Rehana, listen to me. You're very good. You're fast and you're determined. If you follow my rules and you work harder than you ever have before, you can go all the way to the top. I can see it in you. You can take a world junior medal next year. After that we'll look at senior competition." He paused and looked hard into her face. "The 1500 metres is your best event. There's a chance you'll be able to run it in a few years." International athletics committees did not yet recognise the 1500 metres as a women's event. "If you go on running the way you are now, you'll break 4 minutes."

Even Bob had never said that. No one really believed that a woman could run 1500 metres in under 4 minutes. He touched her hand. He spoke perfect English and his accent was light, in the way her father's had been. "I'm sorry about your parents. How are you coping?"

"Okay," she said, though for a moment she was sad. He squeezed her palm. "I know you live on your own. Come and have dinner with us tonight. I cook good Danish food - no bacon."

She laughed. Muslims did not eat pork. He watched her get her coat. There was something about her that made him feel he'd hit the jackpot. She was going to make history one day.

3

David Rae was eighteen years old. His singular aim in life was to win a gold medal at the Olympic Games in the middle distance event he loved best: the 1500 metres.

David was of pure English stock. He had spent his life in the white suburbs of Kent, until finding a job and a bedsit in London. If somebody had asked him about Muslims, David would have shaken his head and not had a clue. He had no idea where Karachi was, and certainly did not know that it had once been part of India. In fact, he had never met an Asian in his life and had no feelings about them one way or the other. What he did know about, aside from athletics, was the music of the Beatles. When George Harrison played sitar on 'Rubber Soul' David thought Asian culture must be beautiful. He also began to see Britain's black and brown citizens in the streets as he explored the capital city. He was intrigued in January 1966 when a woman became Prime Minister of India. He could not imagine that happening in England. With that fresh in his mind, he went along to Finchley Athletics Club to see if he could join. He was amazed to see an Asian girl on the track. She smiled as he passed by her. She had long black hair and dark lashes. Her eyes were warm and he thought she was a very good reason for joining the club.

Peter gave David Rae a test and could scarcely believe the boy's time. Without hesitation he made David Rehana's training partner, right there on David's first day at the club. But he did take them to one side to issue a warning.

"I want you both to be friends, no more. You're going to be training together for the next ten years if I have my way. Don't let anything interfere with that."

Rehana looked at her new friend and saw mock horror in his eyes. She turned away so Peter did not catch her giggling. It was an issue he had never discussed with her before. When he walked away David grinned.

"Is he always that strict?"

"Always. Come on, I'll show you round the club."

Had it not been for Peter's concern, David would have asked her to go out with him. He looked good alongside her. He was tall and slim with straight hair the colour of copper. With his easy smile and wicked humour he loved the thought of being in her life. As they got to know each other better, he and Rehana became almost like brother and sister, spurring each other on to race and win. Obsessed, Peter pushed them harder. With David Rae and Rehana Hassan he had the cream of England's junior runners in his care.

In the summer of 1966 Rehana could not stop thinking of her little sister. Civil rights hero James Meredith was shot in Mississippi and Rehana wondered if Sana really would have grown up to join the struggle. She would be fifteen now, a star of Swinging London. "A little Marxist," Aftar had jokingly called her, but Sana was deadly serious. When the National Guard moved in on the black protesters, Rehana was glad her sister was not there to see it. Sometimes, Peter asked her if she wanted to talk about her family. She said no, for fear it would make her break down. She had sold herself to only one goal and had to be in one piece to get there.

She was on the threshold of well earned success. The Finchley press dubbed her a princess when she won the 800 metres world junior silver at the end of 1966. She wished it had been in the 1500 but continued to build on her success. At the European Junior Championships in Stuttgart, West Germany, Rehana won silver and David gold. They both set national junior records. Returning to England, they got a tremendous boost when the local council voted to pay their living and training costs. They would live on low budgets but could give up their jobs to concentrate on becoming senior champions.

For some time Peter had thought about sending Rehana and David to the 1968 Mexico Olympics. They both made the squad but David had to leave his friend behind. Rehana got a virus two weeks before the Games. Her body had let her down for the first time when it really mattered. She cried for days. It was damned unfair; it was also an enormous test. She had to shake off the bitter misery and get motivated for future senior glory. David kissed her good-bye, believing he might get bronze. Instead, with Peter's coaching and his own guts and faith, he came home with an Olympic silver medal and a new European record. As David made the national press, so did his training partner. Peter was not marketing one without the other. She began to receive limited coverage, always with her name misspelt, always referred to by colour or race. By now she was an adult competitor of twenty one and she almost caught her East German rival at the European Indoor Championships. She became well known in athletics circles and was featured in "Athletics Weekly". But the general public could not yet put a face to the name.

4

West Ham Football Club was celebrating its good sense at signing Andrew Raymond, a Glasgow mid-fielder. Within weeks he was scoring terrific goals. Andrew was twenty three. He dreamed of playing for Rangers but was glad for the chance to try his hand at English football along the way. When Andrew scored goals at Upton Park, girls screamed his name. He was almost better looking than Bobby Moore, with blond hair and cheeky blue eyes. And he had a great body.

West Ham were at a party thrown by a London sportswear company in January 1969. Some of London's promising runners were there too and Rehana Hassan, holder of the national junior record and world junior silver, easily justified her invitation. In the all-white crowd the brown girl with long black hair stood out. She noticed with irritation that some people were staring at her. Andrew did not stare out of prejudice. He was looking at her with desire. He manoeuvred his way across to her and held out a glass.

"Hi, can I tempt you?"

She shook her head. "No, thank you." She was getting used to meeting other athletes, but a footballer was something else. She thought he was just passing, but he stayed beside her.

"You must be an athlete. You were over with Dave Rae."

"Yes. My name is Rehana."

"Rehana." He pronounced it slowly, letting it roll off his tongue. "What a beautiful name."

"Thank you."

"I'm Andrew."

She held back a laugh. "I think I know who you are."

He looked surprised. He was not very famous. "You know football?"

"I love it," she said, and he began to forget about the wine.

"Uh, what's your event, Rehana?"

"800 metres."

"Are you winning?"

"I'm on my way."

When people started to leave, Andrew was still deep in conversation with the runner. His mostly legless team mates drifted away and the athletes followed.

"How are you getting back?" he asked her.

"I have my car outside."

"Oh." He looked disappointed. "I'll walk you to it."

Andrew stood by her Mini and felt quite shy.

"I've had a great evening, Rehana." He shifted around on the path. "How would you feel about getting together again?"

"I'd love to."

"Oh great." He scrambled for his pen. "Here, I'll give you my number. Give me yours."

Their first date brought cool comments from the rest of his team. When Andrew took her out a second time he faced open jibes, about curry and Enoch Powell. Enoch

Powell was a British politician who predicted blood on the streets if dark-skinned immigrants kept coming in. He made Andrew feel sick.

"Andy, a friendly word," his coach Rob Justin muttered. "There are a lot of white girls - lovely girls - who would kill to go out with you. They're also big West Ham loyalists. Don't alienate them."

"Thank you for your friendly advice, Rob," Andrew spat back. "If you'll excuse me, I have a date to get to."

He heard somebody shout, "Don't get curry breath!" and nearly turned back. Then he realised he would be late, and he definitely did not want to be.

In the first month of their relationship, Rehana and her footballer boyfriend became lovers. With the death of her parents she had lost a link with Islam. Though the void was filled a little by their friends, and letters from family in Pakistan, she was already open to another kind of life, one that did not have to include virginity. Twenty one years of belief were not easy to put aside. Muslim girls stayed pure until marriage, and to be a good Muslim but sleep with Andrew too she had to marry him. That was not on. Her base was in London with Peter, while Andrew had to go wherever his next transfer took him. Islam did not give her much choice, and she chose to be bad.

It was a short and exhilarating time. At the end of the 1969 soccer season, Andrew cheerfully turned his back on his racialist team mates and returned to Glasgow for a dream signing with Rangers. Rehana found it hard to be without him, but she had him as a friend. She was in hard training for the 1970 Commonwealth Games and that had to take priority.   She was much too preoccupied to seriously date other men, and had moved to a new flat in Golders Green, not far from Peter's Hampstead home. Golders Green was a suburb of Jews and of kosher stores. There were a few Asians there too.   Rehana kept beef and milk in her upstairs apartment, occasionally sneaking to the Taj Mahal for a rare greasy feast.

5

THE 1970s

Edinburgh was the step from quiet perseverance and gradual wins into not only national but international fame. Rehana was twenty two, brown and representing England with the flag of St George on her vest. It was not a common sight in those days. One day, to be dark and British might be okay in athletics. In 1970 that was a dream. Every step of the way she had to justify her British identity and prove her place in the nation.

Edinburgh was wet and windy, making it tough for new records to be produced. The rain hit the track and the runners' faces at the start of the women's 800 metres race. Some of the English sporting press believed Rehana Hassan had a good chance of gold, but the crowd and most of the media did not know the young British Asian well and were watching Australia and Canada in expectation of a White Commonwealth win. There was an outside chance that the dark-skinned English girl could perform. No one was terribly motivated to support an unknown runner, but of the three Britons in the race Rehana was the only one with her tactics right. When the Finchley girl won, the British press was thrown into chaos. She had just set a Commonwealth record. No one but 'The Guardian' had a profile prepared. It was the only paper that got her birthplace right and did not call her "Asian-born".

Coming off the track in disbelief, she met 'The Guardian' sports journalist Kevin Sommerton. He was young and it impressed her that he wrote for a national newspaper, especially a quality one. Kevin interviewed her in a local wine bar, over orange juice and nuts. He marvelled at the interest she took in his work.

A friendship was formed that day in Edinburgh. Rehana was fortunate that before her international career took her to the front pages of every paper in Europe and much of the world, she had a journalist friend she could trust to report only the truth about her life and beliefs.

The achievements made by the British teams at Edinburgh ensured immediate star treatment for several of the athletes. Most of Scotland's sports fans immediately warmed to Rehana. Stuart Linton of the 'Glasgow Herald' wrote: "There is a naturalness about this twenty two year old runner that charms those around her. She does not shun the press, provided the questions are about her sport. She is loath to discuss her private life and her Pakistani heritage, saying that she is just a runner. Thanks to the efforts of Hassan and her friend Dave Rae England has done superbly at the Games. Anyone who doubts Hassan's ability to win the gold medal at the Munich Olympics in two years' time, when she should have truly peaked, is deluding himself. Edinburgh has seen the birth of a world champion."

Later in the Commonwealth year, Rehana and David went on to win the Stockholm European Championships. In the same week the International Olympic Committee - the all-powerful IOC - voted to allow women to run the

1500 metres at the 1972 Munich Games. Rehana was over the moon.

Since Edinburgh people had begun to stop her in public. It was a strange feeling at first: embarrassing. Her close friend, Kim Fry, who had won silver in the 400 metres, faced the same treatment. Peter had seen it all happen with David and told them they would gradually become used to it, but Rehana felt her fame made her different to people who otherwise wanted the Asians to get out, and she never quite felt comfortable. Going out with Andrew, before they both became famous, had sometimes been rough. Society really did not like mixed race romance and they had often been shouted at in the street. Rehana envied her white friends, who could go on a date without comment.

Aside from race, Rehana was also acutely aware of the politics surrounding religion. It was a time of Palestinian terrorism, matched in Muslim eyes by Israel's repression of a people who had lost their land. She said very little about it but did not hesitate to condemn the hi-jackings that gained the release of the terrorist Leila Khaled. Supporting Palestine did not mean supporting acts of terror. Peter did not want her to talk publicly about those things, but she was the only famous Muslim in Britain and the press was making the most of that.

But athletics came first. The goal was Olympic gold. She was in superb health and full of determination to win. She would be twenty four in the Olympic year, at her peak. Her hours revolved around her running, but when Peter's back was turned she still ran to have a night out with friends at the rock concerts she loved. She

unconsciously made a political statement by seeing George
Harrison and Eric Clapton at the concert for Bangladesh
and had to apologise to Peter when it made the papers the
next day. He wanted her to get covered only for her
running, and Bangladesh was an emotive subject. The
people were fighting for independence from West
Pakistan. Rehana was in extra trouble with Peter for
being too tired to get up to train. Secretly though, he
smiled. His strictness masked the affection he felt for her.

When Britain's Olympic team for 1972 was named, the
press noted that in the athletics squad, six of the women
were unattached, while almost all of the men were
married or engaged. David himself had just married the
Northern Irish swimmer Linda McNeal and Rehana had
become quite close to her. In the climate created by the
sexual revolution of the 1960s almost all public figures
had their private lives scrutinised by the less upmarket
British press. Rehana had kept her relationship with
Andrew as private as possible and only her close friends
knew much about the men she dated. She had offended
some members of the Asian community by being seen in
public with Western men, but she made no excuses. She
was not interested in racial or religious purity where love
was concerned.

Shortly before flying to Munich she was interviewed
for a lengthy profile by Kevin Sommerton. He asked her
not only about running but about her politics as well. She
spoke about her religion and admitted that, although she
prayed and respected the Qu'ran, she had misgivings
about the role of women in most religious practices.
Kevin asked her about Palestine. She said again that

terrorism would not bring land back to the people. But Britain was less concerned with Middle East terrorism than its own state of siege created by the IRA. There was not a lot of joy in the world. For a few hours, sport could change that. Kevin turned off the tape recorder.

"You can relax now. This is off the cuff."

He asked if she hoped to get a good look at West Germany while she was out there. Munich had much to offer. She got up to say good-bye and said,

"I hope you enjoy the country, Kev. I'm just going out there to run."

Three weeks later, Kevin looked back on that comment and did not know how to assess the Munich Olympic Games.

6

The days leading up to the flight were for training only. Over the years Peter Andersen's reputation had grown and he was now charged with coaching several of the team. He was responsible for their ambassadorship to West Germany and their performance for the viewing hundreds of millions, but his foremost ambition was for his two Finchley runners to win Olympic gold.

Rehana took it easy the morning before the flight. She set her stop watch in Golders Hill Park and ran across the grass, feeling the air on her face and the waft of breakfast from the park café. It was not yet 6.30 and most of Golders Green was asleep. Colourful bushes had sprung up around her and the grass was sweet. Elm trees lined the path from the park to the end of the hill.

"Good morning, Rehana," the milkman said, as she made her way back to her flat. She smiled and took her pint of milk up to her kitchen. "Don't forget to cancel for the next two weeks," she called out. The milkman moved on, pleased. It was not every day he encountered the famous athlete. He glanced at the local paper flung across a neighbouring doorstep. In bold print on the front page was a good luck message to Golders Green's star runner.

The team left for Munich on July 26th, a day when London experienced pure summer. They joked about the sun coming out to wish them luck, and laughed on the coach to Heathrow. They buried their nerves in idle chatter; despite the butterflies, it was a wonderful time.

The hit record 'Morning Has Broken' was on the radio, a song of new beginnings. It was as though their lives were starting that day as they headed for the special fiesta that was the Olympic Games. They checked in for their British Airways sponsored flight amid immense security. As they left the VIP lounge, they were submerged in press hysteria, laughing as cameras flashed and questions were shouted out. They were unused to the new security checks. Those were the days when hi-jacks were just beginning, and it was hard to take the threat seriously. Before long they were seated in the plane for the short flight to southern West Germany. They landed in a city full of parties, surrounded by scarves of the Bayern München football team and the beer Peter had forbidden them to drink. But they saw little of the Bavarian capital on the coach ride to the Olympic Park.

It was a breathtaking sight. The silver cobweb of the Olympiastadion looked magnificent before them. As they pulled into the Village they were relaxed by a warm breeze. They embarked on to the tarmac that led to their quarters. The press followed, seeking quick last minute photographs before the official opening of the Games the next day. Steering clear of cameras, Rehana and Kim, rooming together, collected the keys to their flat. It was sparse but had what they needed. No one on the team was living a star's life, and no one expected it. Kim took out a clean tracksuit. Everyone at the Games was invited to a huge buffet under a tent, in the centre of the Olympic Village, to meet fellow competitors.

"Are you dressing for this buffet?" Kim asked.

"I didn't think of it." Rehana lifted a white T-shirt and jeans out of her case. "It's only a casual thing."

"Well, I can't be bothered, I'm exhausted. You'll look okay in that."

They showered before descending to the lobby. The rest of the athletes were already there and Peter pointed to his watch.

"You two are five minutes late. Come on, quickly." It was a light-hearted reprimand. They were all keen to get on with the evening and eventually fall into bed. Tonight, training was out.

Rehana felt calm that evening as she sipped a glass of orange and mixed with the world's top sportsmen and women, especially the Pakistani team. She looked for her American friend Neal Birch and found him surrounded. That was no surprise; Neal held the world record for the 400 metres hurdles. This was his first Olympics too. For some time, he and Rehana had been long distance friends. Neal, born in Georgia into segregation, had actually marched with Martin Luther King. When Rehana touched him on the shoulder he swerved round to hug her. They stood aside over soft drinks and salad in a vain attempt to cut off the hordes of press. Over 4,000 were gathered in Munich and they all seemed to be present tonight.

"Rana, you look great. Peter still driving you hard?"

"I can't breathe," she laughed. As if on cue she turned to see Peter watching her. Caught out in his vigilance, he smiled and looked away.

"He's on wine," she said. "He won't let anyone else touch it."

"You can't stay off booze in Munich!" He grimaced as a camera grazed his cheek. "Look at them. They're like a bunch of hound dogs." He turned his thoughts to sport. "You're going to win this one, Rana."

"I'm running against Ute Brauer."

Brauer, an East German, had been Rehana's biggest threat for years. There was a widespread, but unspoken, fear that the Soviet bloc states were using drugs to enhance their chances. Neal frequently thanked God that his rivals were African.

"You just beat her in Stockholm," he reassured his friend. "It'll be an even stronger victory when you beat her here."

"I hope so," Rehana said. "I know you'll be getting gold!" Her Geordie team mate Paul Kerr was fervently chasing Neal, but really did not have a chance.

As Neal got pulled away by 'The New York Times', Rehana saw Kim come over with two glasses of ice cold water.

"Thanks, this is just what I wanted."

"I was talking to Kev Sommerton, he just got in. He's trying to get Dave."

"No chance. I didn't know he was coming over so early."

It was dusk. While she talked to Kim, a broad shouldered young man in shorts came towards her. It was his T-shirt she noticed first; Hebrew letters circling the Star of David. She looked up to see the face of the athlete and saw the most handsome face she had ever seen. He was smiling, his eyes dancing with her own.

"Hi, I'm Sam Goldberg." His accent was soft. "I hear you're a fellow runner?"

They all laughed. Of course she was - the whole world of sport knew that. Rehana looked at his olive skin and had a shocking urge to touch him.

"Hi," was all she could say. She was beginning to feel the heat.

"I wanted to meet you," he said. "You and some of your team are quite famous in Israel."

Israel. A name synonymous for her with oppression.

"What are you running in?" she replied.

"In the 800."

"With Mick." Her team mate Mick Hall was battling Kenya in that event. He looked intently at her. He was studying her face.

"It's a great feeling to be here," he said. "I've never raced in a world contest before."

Rehana thought about Israel's progress in track and field. He was right - she had never met an Israeli athlete before. "Where are you from?" she asked him.

"Tel Aviv now, but I was born in Haifa. The training facilities are better in the cities."

She did not know what to say next. She was looking for common ground and said, "I live near a synagogue."

Sam smiled and answered, "I live near a mosque." That broke the ice. Rehana was sure afterwards that at that moment, when they broke into laughter, an immense attraction and bond was born between them.

He promised to see her tomorrow. Was he making a date in the sports field? She had come to Munich to run, and now it was her heart that was running.

The night passed quickly and Rehana went out to practice early the next day. She returned to her room to wash and dress before going to the British dining hall. There was a strenuous day ahead. Tonight was the opening ceremony, but only after eight hours of push ups and runs. She passed Peter in the corridor and said she was on her way to breakfast. When she got to the front of the hall she found Sam Goldberg there.

"You've already been out running," he smiled.

"How did you know?" She did not want to show how great it felt to see him. There was a conflict between her sudden desire for him and her feelings about his country.

"Ah, I came here half an hour ago. Rehana, would you take breakfast with us, in our quarters?"

She wanted to say no - it angered her that Palestine did not have an Olympic team - but she had to say yes. "Yes? That's great! Let's go."

He let his feelings show. He probably did not realise that, even as she struggled against it, she felt exactly the same way.

The Israeli quarters were on the other side of the grounds, beyond the tent. They walked easily, if not a little expectantly, taking in the fresh air and talking of the events ahead.

"Everyone will be pleased to meet you," Sam said. "We don't have a world class runner in our team yet."

"This is your chance. You're in the qualifiers next week, alongside my friend, Mick. You've got a very good team out here."

They turned towards the block.

"Your friends call you Rana. May I?"

She smiled and said yes, of course he could. She was making herself remember that he was not responsible for the policies of Israel. He opened a door. "Here we are. Come in and try a real Israeli breakfast."

He introduced her to his close friends; young men, keen to make Israel a serious world competitor. Rehana felt incredibly at ease with the men around her. They were concerned with their training but far more relaxed than anyone in Peter's entourage could afford to be. With a plate of salad before her, and a yoghurt drink she had never tasted, Rehana relaxed with Sam and his closest team mates, Amir and Benjamin. They persuaded her to return that evening. She looked at her watch and said it was time she did some serious training. Sam offered to walk her back.

"Have you come to Germany before?" he asked.

"Only for a junior race. Have you?"

They were moving on to a topic she knew could cause him pain. "No, but I stopped in Austria once, for a few days. My grandparents were from Vienna."

That meant something, but she was not sure if she should ask what. Sam was going to give her the answer anyway.

"I've read interviews about you," he said. "You know a lot about history."

"What happened to your grandparents in Austria, Sam?"

"My grandmother got out," he said slowly, "but my grandfather didn't make it. You know where we believe he died? In Dachau - just down the road."

He paused to look down at the grass of Munich. Rehana touched his arm as he gave a cold laugh.

"In this country," he said.

"Sam," she said quietly, "do you think it's right, what Israel is doing to the Palestinians?" She had to ask. Sam and his friends had all been in the Israeli army, and she had to know what he believed. Did he really think, as some Israelis did, that all Palestinians were the enemy?

"No, I don't," he said to her great relief. "If I did, do you think I would be chasing you? I believe we can all live together."

He grasped her hand at the door of her block. They would eat together that evening, after the opening ceremony. For the rest of the day they both had to train and get used to the climate and surroundings.

At the 1968 Olympics over 200 Mexican students were reported killed in the run-up to the Games. The authorities in Munich remembered that, and wished the world to remember their turn as a celebration. Politics was not in the programme. The Olympic Committee aim was to strengthen friendship between the sportsmen and women of all nations, though for Palestine there was no such chance. Thank God Sam shared Rehana's view.

The two hundred plus members of the Great Britain team - track and field, swimmers, and many more - were to walk into the stadium in red, white and blue. Rehana and Kim chuckled as they left their room to see David, Paul and Mick hovering outside in blue suits.

"You girls look just as silly as us," Mick teased.

"I can't get used to this tie," Paul said. "I'll be glad when this is over."

David looked at his training partner. Almost all of the time they were together, Rehana had her tracksuit or running vest on. This evening she was transformed by her blue skirt and jacket and white blouse. He playfully tugged at her red bow tie, knowing she did not want to wear it.

"Let's get going," he said. They stopped for a moment as Peter came their way. He looked ill at ease, disliking ceremonies and tense about his athletes' image.

"Have a drink, Peter," Mick suggested.

"I've had one." Peter buttoned his jacket. "The world is going to be looking at you. Have a good time but take care."

Walking into the Munich stadium was an experience they would never forget. The whole world was watching. Television pictures were supplied by West Germany's ZDF, but British TV ran its own commentary. It made special mention of Rehana Hassan and David Rae, but so did every other television network. Stations across the world were at that moment highlighting the world's two most popular middle distance runners. Though Rehana was not yet world champion, the public had already put her there. In Pakistan her relatives watched with enormous joy. Pakistan television had devoted special live coverage to the moment she entered the forum. They loved Rehana over there, even though she was not running for them. The Muslims in India felt they had a stake in her too. They regretted the fact that she was born one month after her parents' slice of India became Pakistan. The young fans of sport at home in Britain watched their idols wave tiny Union Jacks. For the black children growing up to racialist abuse, Rehana was the biggest boost they could have.

The Israeli team was not very far behind Great Britain. It had eight athletes and two officials and marched in to the polite applause reserved for unknowns. There was no shame in the clapping. It occurred to no one that those men were marching in the land that had gassed and shot many members of their families. Rehana looked round for Israel when her team took its place, but there were hundreds of heads in the way. She would have loved to hear the athletes talking in their Hebrew language. It was similar to Arabic, the language in which she prayed, and she sometimes heard it on the streets of Golders Green. The suburb's Jews walked to the synagogue near Rehana's flat every Saturday. On many Christian sabbaths, when the Jewish shops were open, Rehana would pop into the kosher store near her street to chat with its owners and purchase beef. Daniel and Lita would be watching her on TV now. They had pinned her Edinburgh victory photograph on to a community notice board inside the shop.

As Israel stood behind the Irish team, Sam whispered to his friend Amir, "I've never met such a beautiful girl. In the flesh she's stunning, and so warm, Amir."

"I know how you feel, but concentrate on your running! There's plenty of time to get to know her after this."

"Oh yeah? I'll invite you to the wedding." He grinned.

"You really mean it, don't you?" Amir said. "Are you sure she wants you?"

"No problem. I've looked into her face; she's going to marry me."

The crowd roared as the flame of the 20th Olympic Games was lit, spreading endurance and friendship across the stadium. Waldi the Dachshund, the symbol of the Games, was illuminated. The world was having fun. As soon as it was over Sam went looking for his girl. She was talking to David, telling him about her meeting with Sam and breakfast with his team, and David was intrigued. What kind of a man could have such an effect on his friend? He saw Sam coming towards her. Amid hundreds of athletes returning to the flats, they met for the first time.

"Did you enjoy it?" Sam asked.

"It was great." Rehana had again that desire to hold him. "Sam, this is David."

"Great to meet you, David," Sam said. For a minute he was lost for words. He held out his hand and David took it warmly. "You're in the 800? Good for you."

"Well, I have to qualify first."

"You'll make it fine. I hear Shaki's a very good coach."

"He's tough on us, yeah." Sam touched Rehana on the arm as somebody called David away. "I can't believe I just talked to David Rae. I need to go for a walk. Come on, you can teach me a few running tactics as well."

Out of sight of the athletes, Sam felt his feelings running ahead of him.

"Rana, may I hold your hand?"

"Yes." She smiled as he held it firmly. "Sam, I looked for you. I guess Israel was a few teams behind us. Did you see Neal?"

"Neal Birch?"

"Yes. He wasn't sure about coming."

"No, I didn't see him. What are we talking about?"

"I don't know." Rehana turned and put her arms round him. "I can't think of anything to say."

Sam responded by kissing her.

"You don't have to say anything," he said. "I know what you feel."

"Do you think this was planned for us?"

"Yes. Fate is a silly concept until it happens to you."

"I kept thinking of you out there," Rehana said.

"I kept thinking of you. You see?" He stroked her hair. "When the Games are over I'm going to marry you."

She laughed lightly at that, but knew he was serious. It did not seem ridiculous at all. Only a week earlier she would have scorned the possibility of this happening.

They ate together in the Israeli block. Over a kosher meal and light German bread they talked of each other's lives. Benjamin and Amir sat at their table, pressing Rehana for news of her famous team mates.

"Hey, Rehana," Amir teased, "do you know the Hebrew word for love?"

"It's 'ahava'," Benjamin said. "It's what's coming out of Sam's eyes."

They all laughed as Sam reached over to punch his friend. Their coach Chaim Shaki came over.

"Sam, you should let this young lady go. Take her back to her flat; you all have to get up early to practice."

"Chaim, you're spoiling his fun," Amir protested.

"He's got plenty of time for fun after he's run for his country. And Miss Hassan has to sleep too. I know Peter Andersen's reputation."

"We should be in school," Sam groaned. "Okay Coach, you win."

"Don't take too long walking her back," Chaim said. He pressed Rehana's shoulder. "Come and eat with us again."

Returning to the block, Sam telephoned his brother in Tel Aviv. Abraham said that Israeli television had just run a film about its team.

"How is it over there Sam? It looks beautiful on TV."

"I've fallen for somebody. I think she feels the same way about me."

His brother shook his head.

"You know, you're out there to race, not fall in love! Who is it, a runner?"

"It's Rehana Hassan."

"Oh God - Sam be careful." Abraham saw the headlines before him. For the first time he wished his little brother was not the great risk taker they all admired.

"We'll be fine," Sam answered. "No one's bothered about politics here, Abi."

"Not at the Olympics maybe, but - "

"Tell everyone. I want them to be prepared when I bring her over to meet you."

At that moment Rehana and Kim were talking into the night. They should have been getting some sleep, but Kim was after a run down.

"He's romantic, Rana," Kim said, excited by her friend's full account. "He sounds fantastic."

"I've never felt so good before. I think I really love him."

"God - what a thing to happen when you're going for an Olympic medal. This is brilliant."

At breakfast, Kevin Sommerton approached Rehana at her table. "You're looking happy."

"Sit down," she said. "Have a coffee."

"Thank you. I want you to confirm a rumour I heard."

"What is it?" She seemed amused.

"Just a bit of gossip. I hear you've struck up a friendship with a runner from Israel, Samuel Goldberg."

"That's right."

"The gutter press are going to have a field day."

She put down her cup. "I don't read what the gutter press say."

"It's a very interesting story, Rana. A Muslim and an Israeli, especially with what you've said on Palestine. What does he say about that?"

"Oh come on, Kev, we're representing our countries in sport, not politics. Do you have to ask about that?"

"Other people are going to."

Rehana felt irritated for the first time. "Other people don't need to know. I don't ask Sam about his religion and he doesn't ask me."

"I think you should start to care," Kevin said. "I don't want to see you upset."

She was touched by his concern. "Kev, I only want to read your kind of journalism. I don't want politics brought into this. We're just going to concentrate on our running and try and have a good time as well."

It was the last naïve statement she would make. Until then, Rehana and Sam never thought their relationship could make news when world records were being broken around them. Later that day, after lengthy training sessions, Rehana met Sam outside his block and they walked towards the quieter side of the grounds. They heard a noise behind a bush and looked round into a camera.

"Can I get one more?"

He was British.

"How many have you taken?" Sam asked light-heartedly.

"Just the one. I need a couple."

"Why?" Rehana was afraid he was from one of the rags.

"Oh come on, Rehana, it's a scoop. I'll give you the paper when it's out."

Sam smiled. "Okay, my friend. Here's one just for you." He took Rehana's hand and they stood still for five seconds before walking away. "They just want a bit of light relief," Sam said. "It's good fun for the media."

They spent half an hour together until Rehana saw David coming towards her.

"Sorry, Rana, Peter wants us all back in the block."

Sam jokingly held her back.

"I have to go," she laughed.

"Okay, I won't keep you. I just realised I haven't told you I love you."

"I love *you*." She had said it at last. He kissed her and gently broke away.

"Go on."

She watched him walk away and wanted to scream out with joy.

"Hey, don't I get a kiss too?" She felt David's arm round her.

"You?" She kissed her friend on the cheek. "Come on."

The next morning, the London 'Daily Mail' sports headline read: 'Love at the Olympics - Rehana and handsome Israeli.' The paper said she had a lot more on her mind at the Olympic Games than winning a gold medal.

The rest of the media seized on the story that day, and Rehana and Sam found themselves pursued by reporters and photographers across the Village. British reporters began trailing their star athlete between her training sessions, asking her if she and Mr Goldberg would become engaged. She gave no reply to such foolish questions, but her smile meant a great deal. She and Sam answered questions politely but with surprise. They had not realised how their romance, short as it was, could so greatly boost the sales of papers and magazines outside sport. Rehana had always thought that was reserved for movie stars. It was laughable, but it did not stay that way for long.

Peter and Chaim were uncomfortable and asked Rehana and Sam not to court unnecessary publicity. They accepted that, and turned down an invitation for a press conference. Besides, they did not think they had anything to say. ZDF, however, chased Rehana after an early evening run and asked her on live TV what plans she had with Sam when the Games ended. At that moment she felt completely in love - with Sam and with Munich - but she remembered Peter's caution and said only, "We are very good friends." Frustrated, ZDF followed Sam to his block and breached poor security to get inside. Sam, unused to press attention, was a little easier to interview. He was still enjoying the novelty of it all.

"We are two people who have just become friends and find they have a very special relationship," he said. "We don't talk about the future, there's plenty of time. Above all we're here to run, and it's like a holiday romance, though we are very serious. It's a real bond, a bond of friendship."

"What about your religious differences, Sam?" ZDF asked.

Sam gave the question some thought and replied with the confidence of those who put love before doctrine, "What does it matter? We both believe in God."

But others did not see it that way.

On Day Six of the Games, Peter opened one of the many letters arriving for Rehana Hassan. He paled as he looked at the death threat before him. It was what he had feared. He conferred with British team official Geoff Steele and they decided not to let Rehana know. Peter sought out Chaim Shaki in the privacy of his rest room.

Chaim was on edge as he read the note, and said he wished Sam had thought ahead.

"Jew and Muslim - it doesn't work. How can it?"

Peter said nothing. Chaim looked at him for a moment, and continued. "She is a lovely girl, but what do her family think about this?" He closed his eyes briefly. "Sam is a romantic. He saw her on TV in Israel and he wanted to meet her. He's let it go too far."

Peter reached for a glass of water. The blocks were poorly ventilated, and there was no window in Chaim's parlour.

"Rehana doesn't have a family, Mr Shaki," he said. "If Sam is the right man for her, I don't think that religion should come into it." He crumpled the note into a litter bin. "I hope it's just a scare tactic," he murmured. "I don't want those two hurt."

He shook hands with Sam's coach - he respected Chaim for building a quality team - and walked on to the balcony. It was too humid for fresh air, and his head felt heavy. By early evening his athletes only wanted to sleep. It was much warmer than anyone had expected; even nervous energy could not keep them awake.

Rehana was talking to Mick and Paul when Peter asked her to walk with him. By his silence she could tell he was tense. They stopped a few yards away from the others and, though he knew she would not, he advised her to put her romance on hold. "Just be careful, Rana," he said with unusual tenderness. "There's plenty of time for you and Sam to be together after the Games."

He said no more, but when she looked into his face there was an expression of anxiety she rarely saw in him.

Sam was training and had put everything else out of his head when Chaim came over to him.

"Sam, I think we should talk." There was a warning in his coach's voice and Sam knew what was coming. Chaim was not angry, but there was definitely a lecture on the agenda. "A lot of people don't understand it, Sam. Remember you're a Jew."

"So what, Chaim?" Sam said quietly. "It's possible for different religions to exist together."

"Right now? With all this killing?"

"Why not? Somebody has to challenge it. We don't just live in the Middle East, we live in the world."

Chaim gave a deep and irritated sigh. "It's not a world that is as tolerant of differences as you are, Sam."

"Chaim, it's no good." Sam was mad at being patronised. "I love her."

By Day Seven, world reaction to Rehana and Sam became apparent. In some quarters there was outrage. Newspapers and gossip magazines were caught up in judgement, and an Israeli journalist present said he was shocked at the openness of Sam's love for a Muslim. Chaim listened and would not comment. He knew that what Sam did should be no one else's affair, but he was not shocked at the evidence around him that the world did not easily accept inter-racial love. Muslim commentators at Munich, especially those from Pakistan, were offended to see the two athletes holding hands. In Israel it would be hard for Sam to find acceptance of his pro-Palestinian girlfriend. His friends had all served in the Israeli army and would all have something to say. His parents might tolerate his choice of wife but would never really come

round to it. Loving Rehana meant he would always have
to take care. He would have to defend his love,
something which he felt he should not have to do.
Chaim's warning was only the beginning of it. He could
not imagine what the people in Israel were saying.

On the same day, a Pakistani newspaper published an
article that incensed every one of Rehana and Sam's
friends. The publishers feared Rehana's relationship with
Sam might set an example for the young Pakistani fans of
sport. The text read thus: "Love between members of
different teams in international sports events is not
surprising or remarkable. What is, is the willingness of
the athletes in this case to completely overlook the
implications that their 'bond of friendship' is certain to
have on young people's attitudes. Miss Rehana Hassan is
a Muslim.   Her open relationship with Mr Samuel
Goldberg, an Israeli, is irresponsible. Young people will
begin to ignore the very obvious differences between
faiths if those they idolise act in this way.
Miss Hassan and Mr Goldberg do not appear to realise
the complexities of inter-racial marriage and the effect on
the children of such marriages. It is commendable to
foster good relations with persons of other cultures, but
differences cannot be denied. Miss Hassan is a Muslim
born and raised in Great Britain. She cannot understand
the East. Peace cannot be achieved through random
affairs of the heart, for ultimately the head must rule."

It was deeply hurtful. Peter was astonished by its force
and by the number of other papers which quoted it.

Despite refusing to comment, the article greatly wounded Rehana and Sam; they were stunned by it. Rehana was mad that day, but did not let anyone know. Once the running was over she could maybe say what she felt. Tired, she looked at that morning's 'Guardian'. Kevin rarely commented on the private lives of athletes, but the political climate in the Village had made him stray from that rule. Rehana smiled as she read the familiar style: "Several journalists in the Olympic Village and beyond, are attacking the friendship between Rehana Hassan and Samuel Goldberg. It is not my place to comment on love, but some things need to be said: anyone open-minded enough to see this friendship without relating it to race, or to political events in the Middle East, will only be enriched by the happiness one feels around this resilient couple. If the Olympic spirit of international friendship extends into personal relationships it is no bad thing. In this warring world we can do far worse."

Rehana was grateful that Britain, at least, would read a sane point of view. She told Sam what Kevin had said. He too was tired of the politics.

"Come back to the block with me," he said. "I got you something."

They walked into the room Sam shared with Amir, taking care to leave the door wide open should the press sneak in. It was quiet in the flats. Only Tsachi, a young swimmer, was inside. For him competition was over and he was on his way out for a tour of the city. Sam placed a cassette player on a chair and took a tape from a drawer. He asked Rehana to listen to the one year old hit.

"This is what I felt about you when I saw that stupid article. I don't know how else to tell you."

The music of 'Bread' began gently to fill the room.
The words could have come from Sam's heart.

Hey, have you ever tried
Really reaching out for the other side?
I may be climbing on rainbows
But baby here goes

Dreams, they're for those who sleep
Life is for us to keep
And if you're wondering
What this all is leading to
I want to make it with you

Though you don't know me well
And every little thing only time will tell
If you believe the things that I do
Then we'll see it through

Life can be short or long
Love can be right or wrong
And if I chose the one I'd like to help me through
I'd like to make it with you

I really think that we can make it girl

Afterwards, no words were needed to describe how he
felt. They walked in one of the areas barred to the press,
where only their fellow athletes could see them together.
It became cooler as they crossed the hill and stood in the
grounds close to the medical quarters. Sam spoke of his
grandfather, murdered not far away.

"He was a sprinter. My father says it skipped a
generation and landed in me." He kicked a stone. "I
can't believe he died near this beautiful place."

Rehana pulled her tracksuit top around her, shivering
slightly, but not from cold.

"It's going on right now, all over. It's not history."

Vietnam, Uganda, Burundi - all made the headlines that
year for the deaths of innocent citizens, while the world
did nothing. Sam was right. The sun and beauty of
Munich hid the terrible existence of the village of Dachau
and the camp crematorium just a few train stops away.

1972 meant Bloody Sunday and Idi Amin. Many
unarmed people were dying.

The tenth day of the Games came fast. Rehana came
down to breakfast the morning after a superb semi-final
time to find Mick and Kim poring over 'The Washington
Post'. The paper had dedicated a half page, with
photographs, to the Hassan-Goldberg affair. Quoting
many of the world's press, it stated the silent thoughts of
millions:

"Out of every Olympic Games comes controversy.
This year, the headline makers are an English Moslem
runner Rehana Hassan and one of Israel's new track
athletes, Samuel Goldberg. Hassan and Goldberg have
caused offence in Israel and the Moslem world, where

their unusual closeness draws severe criticism. Though not yet twenty five, they cannot enjoy their love in peace.

London-born Hassan, the daughter of Indian immigrants to Britain in the 1940s, and Goldberg, the Haifa-born grandson of a sprinter murdered in Dachau, make no attempts to conceal their relationship. They are honest and open about it, admitting it is too early to share with us their plans for the future and laughingly calling it a 'holiday romance'. But the Olympic Games are not a holiday resort. Nations can run and compete in harmony, but love affairs between people from different races are not yet kosher in the Olympic arena. Frowns have been raised, despite the alacrity with which the West German media and public have accepted the romance. The West Germans are right. There is something joyous about the way these young people openly hold hands. They are mocking bigotry. The spirit of the Olympics is the promotion and strengthening of friendship between sportsmen and women of all countries. Nowhere does it say that they should not fall in love."

After the pain of the Pakistani article it was just what Rehana needed to see. Mick pushed the paper aside.

"A lot of people agree with that. Forget that other trash. Everyone wants to see you win today."

It was not the only press comment that day in support of the couple. Barbel Dieter of the West German 'Suddeutsche Zeitung' was warm about the romance in her column, voicing the feelings of thousands of Bavarians who had fallen for Rehana and Sam. Sometimes, it was possible to forget what Germany had done to millions.

The moment had finally come. From the day Rehana saw women run middle distance events at the 1960 Rome Olympics on a black and white TV, it had been her dream to do the same. Her spirits lifted, she left the quarters to get a final feel of the track. UK TV cameras were on her, but most of the time she was too nervous to know. She still had the 800 metres to run on Day Twelve, but the 1500 had to be hers. It always had been, since the days with Bob Lewis when her parents were alive and her little sister got in her way. She was going to win. East Germany's Ute Brauer was equally sharp, but she mentally blocked Brauer out.

After a wait, and a quiet chat with Peter, the time arrived. Sam walked with her to the stadium, ignoring the posse of photographers around them.

"I don't think I can bear to watch you," he said.

"You have to." Rehana pushed a camera out of her way. "God, I feel nervous."

"No you don't, you feel confident. You look great and you're going to look great when you have that gold medal round your neck." He laughed suddenly. "You know, this is what you came here for! I just got in the way." He kissed her and she stayed for a moment in his arms. He put dark shades on and wished her good luck as he joined her friends in the stands. If she won it would be Britain's fifth gold medal at Munich and its first on the track.

As the race began, Rehana put her complete faith in Peter and the techniques she had learned in the punishing schedules he mapped out. It would be no easy victory, with Ute on her shoulder and top runners from Australia, the Soviet Union and Italy right behind. Three times she was overtaken in the home straight. Her pacing had been perfect, but this was the time to make the sudden break. Brauer almost got there and Peter's stomach churned. Sam could not look, but David was watching with certainty that she would win. With one tremendous surge in the last 100 metres, Rehana sent her body forward. Her legs almost gave way. In 4 minutes and 8 seconds against Ute's 4 minutes 10, she had won Olympic gold and set a new Commonwealth record.

Somebody in the British part of the crowd reached over to hand her a large Union Jack. Rehana kissed the flag and took it on a victory lap around the track. She fell into Peter's arms.

"You cracked it, darling," he said. "I'm proud of you."

"You trained me," Rehana replied.

The cameras were still on her when she and Sam kissed. He was elated. "I'm so happy for you," he said. "You really deserve it."

Standing with the gold medal around her neck, as the British anthem played, Rehana felt more than elation. It was indescribable. It must surely have been the proudest moment of her life.

The celebration at the British quarters that evening was full of champagne and music, even though Britain's Muslim champion did not drink and Peter had forbidden any remaining runners to give in. Neal Birch came along, and several of Sam's team mates. Kevin was there, the only British reporter with an invitation. Two or three others gatecrashed. Sam had to leave early, to prepare for his semi-final the next day. He was still not sure how he had got that far. Before he left, Neal photographed him with Rehana.

"I'm on tomorrow too, Sam."

"So we wish each other luck." Sam took Neal's hand. "You'll easily win."

"Thanks. I've got to think that too."

"Put your whole heart in it. I'll be backing you."

It was an evening of sheer relief and laughter. Rehana walked across the field with Sam towards the Israeli block, talking about his tactics for the next day, her own 800 metres semi, and David's 1500 metres final. It was 8.30. They passed several friends on the way and stopped to chat. Reaching the mid-way point, and reluctant to part, they walked slowly. It was a warm night. Sam took Rehana's hand. "Can you really love an Israeli?" She laughed, but hollow laughter only. The days of overlooking it were nearing an end. She did not answer. He became serious. He tenderly gripped her by the shoulders. "Listen, you're a Muslim. Muslims don't fall in love with Israelis."

"I've fallen in love with a man." Rehana's voice shook. "Not with a country. I'm not going to answer for that."

"We have to decide what we want, Rana. You know what we've got is much more than friendship."

"I'm not afraid of anyone knowing that."

"Because you want to prove that we can be in love?"

"Because I love you. *You.* Not a religion or a country. Hey, you're not having an affair with Islam."

She wanted to laugh but it never came out. Sam was scared and it scared Rehana to know that.

"Rana, you know it could get worse," Sam said. "We've made headlines for nothing at all. The press love it but there are people around - cranks - who could force us to stop."

"All I want is to love you, and no one can stop that. Come on, we love each other!" She broke out of Sam's arms. Her eyes felt wet. He came and took back her hand.

"I'm sorry," he said. "You know, God made us both. Why shouldn't He want us to love each other?"

They walked together, and in time they started to run, to feel the joy of the grass and the freedom from reality that sport brought. Leaving Sam and returning to her block, Rehana placed her Kodak camera in its case. The film was full of the evening's celebrations. She still had to sleep in order to run well the next day; she would be watching Sam run in the afternoon, and David and Neal as well. It made her feel quite nervous. She sat down on her bed, tired. She still did not fully believe that this rare gold medal was hers. Closing her eyes, she prayed, thanking God for the tremendous luck He had given her. It was time she had a man to love, to help replace the emptiness the deaths of her parents and Sana had brought. She had no doubt that Sam was that man.

But they did not get a chance to take their love beyond borders, towards marriage. The horror of that night cut every bone in her body.

7

David and Paul had risen early. It was 6.00a.m. Somebody knocked on the door as David washed his face, sick at the thought of his 1500 metres run. Paul, thinking of going for a run, rolled off the bed in his shorts and trainers to open the door to Geoff Steele.

"What's going on, Geoff?" he yawned.

"Is David in here?"

"At this hour, yeah. Dave, Geoff's here for you."

David came through, holding his towel. "It's a bit early, isn't it? Don't tell me the race has been brought forward!"

"I have to ask you to do me a very hard favour."

"What's up?"

Geoff could not look directly at him. "This is very bad news. Rehana is going to be badly hit."

David and Paul knew at once that this was no sporting matter.

"Something terrible happened two hours ago," Geoff said. "I would have asked Peter to do this but he's not around."

"What is it?" David was scared.

"Sam Goldberg is dead."

David could not answer. He looked at Paul, as ashen-faced as himself, as Geoff quietly continued. "It's very serious. A group of terrorists broke into the Israeli quarters around four this morning. Two of the athletes - including Sam - were shot dead. The others, and Mr Shaki, are being held hostage. They want a jet out of Munich."

"Oh God." David saw in his mind the faces of Rehana and Sam the night before. "Oh God."

"David, I have to ask you to tell her. I'm sorry. I don't want her to find out from the press; it's better if she hears it from you."

"Yeah, of course." He paused as Paul touched his arm. "Uh, where is Sam?"

"He's been moved with the other dead athlete Amir Pazner, to a room in the medical block."

"Can I see him?"

"Oh David - "

"I've got to, Geoff. I can't tell her until I have."

Sam and Amir lay side by side, covered by white sheets through which blood had soaked. Sam's face was untouched. Amir's was bloodied.

"Mr Goldberg was sprayed in the chest," a doctor said. "Mr Pazner was shot in the back of his head."

"Sam - " David bent and touched the cold face, and repressed the tears welling up in his eyes. How could it have happened? This was the Olympic Games. He made the slowest walk of his life, knowing Rehana would be out on the hill near their block. She had warmed up there every day since coming to the Games. Though he dreaded it, he was relieved Geoff had come to him first. She would be crushed to hear it from anyone except her friends.

Rehana turned when David came towards her. He touched his friend's shoulder. "Rana - " His voice was filled with pain. "I wanted to tell you before the press get to you. There's been a terrorist attack. On the - the Israeli flats." Her paling face must have mirrored his own. She was gripped by stomach pain. "A group of Arabs, they've shot two of the athletes." Tell her, a voice inside his head shouted. "They've got the others hostage."

"Who - who have they shot?"

Her legs were shaking, as on the day her Aunt Lakshmi told her that parents and sister had died. David was white. Could he tell her how Sam had been shot in cold blood, before any chance of negotiation?

"Sam got hit, Rana. He's dead."

"Who told you?" Her voice was broken. *"Who told you!"*

"I - I've seen him, Rana. I'm sorry."

For a long while, David had his arm around Rehana on the grass.

Shock was making her body shake, though at that moment she could not cry. She was silent until she whispered that she wanted to be with Sam.

David told her that Amir had been shot too. He did not want her to go to the makeshift morgue, but she would not let him take her back to her room. She did not really take in the fact that Amir was gone too and he guided her to the room where Sam's corpse lay, still with his friend by his side.

It was his face, Sam's face. His dark brown eyes closed. Dead. Outside, a few of the press had started to gather and word had begun to spread across the outside world that terrorists had infiltrated the Olympic Games. Sam's team mates and Chaim were still inside their quarters, hostages to the hooded and masked Arabs. Rehana had bent to hold Sam's cold hand and could not let it go. There was still so much life in his face. David had never seen her lose control and it hurt him to see her in such pain. In the privacy of the room barred to the press, he embraced his friend as she wept in the cold reality of the Olympics. Peter came in, his face heavy with shock, and took Rehana in his arms behind the closed door. She had lost her strength. Her body felt lifeless. He held her like a father, forgetting the few people around. No one wanted to believe this was really happening. "Take her back to her room and stay with her," he said to David. "I'll keep the press out."

Rehana whispered that she did not want to go. Peter told her that she had to, that there was nothing that could be done. He touched her face and his heart broke to see her red eyes.

David and Kim stayed with her, shunning reporters gathering outside the room. "They want a photo of her," Kim said bitterly.

Neal was out practising, in readiness for his big race. The US camp was on the other side of the Village and news of the massacre was not travelling fast within the grounds. His team mates told him that two Israelis were dead. He found out who and sank to the ground in horror. He threw down his holdall. Kevin, meanwhile, sat in silence in the press room. He had sensed an outrage might happen, and he could not believe the lapse in security. The Games had been suspended. On the other side of the Village, the terrorists were surrounded by TV cameras. Their leaders were having a party.

In the British quarters there was abhorrence, especially among the track athletes. They were irritated by the press outside, hounding every athlete and team official who passed. Against her friends' advice Rehana turned on the

TV and saw the reporters outside her door. She also saw repeated German bulletins on the crisis, which fortunately she did not understand.

At 11.00a.m a jet came to fly the gunmen and hostages to the Furstenfeldbruck military base. Paul and Mick stood outside their rooms and saw Peter come in past the crowd.

"I thought Geoff had come to talk about training," Paul said, his quiet voice still shaking. "What kind of people can kill an athlete?"

"It's politics, Paul," Peter said. "Think about your race. You can't help Rana right now and the Games are going to go on once the rest of the Israelis are freed."

"What if they're not, Peter?" Mick asked. It was horrible to think of the consequences.

"We have to wait. That's all I can tell you."

"Mr Andersen." A reporter came towards him, a microphone round his neck. "Is Rehana in there?"

"No one is going to see her today," Peter replied in acid tone.

"Just a few words for her supporters. I'll be *very* quick."

"No chance, okay? Forget it."

They had never seen Peter so white with anger.

"Come on, Mr Andersen, her fans want to know how she feels. It won't..."

"How she feels!" Peter spun round to face the insufferable young man. "How the hell do you think a girl feels when she's in love and the man gets shot by some terrorists? I'm telling you, you won't see her, she's not seeing anyone from *any* paper. Just get out!"

The reporter saw distaste on Paul and Mick's faces. Mick caught up with Peter as Paul walked away. "Peter, take it easy, those idiots are everywhere. They've got nothing better to do."

"I lost my temper. My God, Mick, she won a gold medal yesterday. What's happening?"

As the morning progressed, the Black September Group of El Fatah - the terrorist organisation holding the Israeli team - telephoned ZDF.

"All the flags at the stadium are now half-mast," the spokesman said. "Where is the Palestinian flag? Where is the Palestinian team?"

The room became claustrophobic, but they would rip her apart if she stepped outside. She had cried a lot. She was trying to close her eyes when Kim answered the extension in their room and said it was Sam's brother. Abi Goldberg knew from the moment he heard Rehana's voice that his brother had chosen the right girl. "I'm flying to Munich tonight," he said. "I want to bring you back here for the funeral and to stay with us. Sam would have brought you. Please come."

It was a hell of a way to see Sam's home. But of course she would. Night came and she fell into a hellish sleep. Right at that moment, a jet arrived at the air base to take the terrorists and hostages out of West Germany. As the terrorists came out towards it, West German marksmen opened fire. It was a hopelessly bungled attempt. A terrorist threw a hand grenade into the hostages' jet, killing them all. As the news reached the Village somebody began to organise a memorial service for the dead.

In the morning no one wanted to eat. Rehana showered to stay awake and left her breakfast on the table. She dressed in slow, mechanical motion and waited for Abi to arrive. Peter heard from Geoff that the Games would remain suspended until the next afternoon. They had to prepare their runners for their finals and attempt to keep a feeling of normality at a time of revulsion.

Abi arrived at Munich, with several of the athletes' relatives. Grief at the sight of the city where their lives had ended was mixed with numbness and disbelief. Officials from the Israeli Embassy in Bonn accompanied the group to the Village. When Abi met Rehana they embraced in tears. She looked at his eyes. He and Sam were alike, separated by only a few years. He took her hand and they sat in her room. It was hard to talk. Abi bowed his head as Rehana described her time with his brother. It was so typical of Sam to enjoy life as he desired. They spent the day together, talking, and pushed past the media scrum to take a walk in the grounds. She learned about Sam's family, and Abi learned about hers. Geoff organised her ticket to Israel, and David and Linda drove to the centre to buy her a dress for the memorial service and funeral. The practical things had to be done. Cameras ruthlessly focused in on her at the Munich service, and she turned her face away.

They were to fly to Israel the next evening. First, the final athletics medals were to be decided. David and Neal were sure to get gold. Mick would run the day after and challenge for gold too. Kim, battling another East German, was looking for silver. Neal was first off, and he set a new world record. He forsook celebration - it did not seem right - and looked for Rehana.

"You've still got the relay to come," she said. She looked at the time. "I forgot to watch you race."

He wanted deeply to comfort her. Grief had made her so small.

"Paul came in third," he said. "He was cut up about running. I guess we all were."

"I'm glad you went ahead. Why should they get another victory?"

"They've got *no* victory, Rana. People hate what they've done. They've set back their cause."

"But it's on the front pages, all over the world!" Rehana thought back to her pre-Munich comments on Palestine. "I supported that cause! We both did. God, one minute he's here and we're laughing, and now - it's just empty. I can't even think about what he went through." She looked through tears at Neal's tracksuit which bore the American flag. "You have to go and get your medal. I'll watch you and Paul on TV."

"Rana - I'm so sorry. I wish..."

"I'll be happy to see you up there. Give me a wave."

David won the 1500 as Neal and Paul prepared to walk to the rostrum. Paul, pipped for silver by Uganda, just could not feel thrilled at his bronze medal. He passed David as the new Olympic champion left the track. Neither was celebrating. Winning meant little right now. Paul took his place on the stand and looked out across the stadium. It was the first medal ceremony after the horror, and the crowd was looking to the athletes to help it forget. Paul leant forward to get his medal and forced a smile.

He was the youngest member of the team and his eyes always laughed. British TV had never seen him keep still.

"Usually you can't keep him down," Peter said. He turned to David and they fell silent. After six years of training for Olympic gold there was no joy to be felt.

Rehana watched on TV as she had promised. Afterwards, ZDF asked Neal for a few words.

"I don't really know what to say," Neal said. "It's a very tragic time and it's a time to celebrate as well. Like that song, you know - a time to laugh, a time to weep. I don't like the contradiction."

"What do you feel about the Games coming on again today? Is it too early?"

"I don't think so; we had to go on. Whatever horror has happened, it does no good to stop a sporting event. We just have to let the terrorists see that we're not moved by what they've done. It's not a happy day."

Rehana turned off the TV set and lay down on the bed. Later, she braved the photographers to go out and support David at his medal ceremony.

"How do you feel, Rehana?" a voice called out.

"What would you say to the terrorists?" shouted another. Her body shook with the strain of the intrusion, but she did cheer up when David got his medal. There was still a lot to be glad about.

Photographers even pursued her to Munich Airport. She got a final hug from David, who was in no mood to be courteous to the press. He told them to go to hell. The Israeli Ambassador accompanied Rehana and Abi and the small group of relatives to Tel Aviv. Rehana saw the coffins taken on to the plane and wanted to pray, but she could not. She sat beside Abi, looking with tired eyes at photographs of Sam's family. They could not sleep. Abi put his arm around her and for most of the flight they sat in silence. They landed at Tel Aviv's Lod Airport. Looking away from cameras, Rehana paused at the site of the Red Army slaughter of twenty six people months earlier. Yet another reminder of Palestine's bloody revenge.

Abi took Rehana to his parents' home. They were desperate to talk, to hear about the final days of Sam's life. Abi's wife Leah was there with their baby son. She recalled Sam's excitement at being an uncle. No one spoke of religion. It would not bring Sam back.

In the morning came the funerals. Behind dark glasses, Rehana saw Sam for the last time and placed the cherished gold medal in his hand. He had flown home to his family, but they could not welcome him with flowers and smiles. As she walked away, her hands were shaking and she was crying. She was thankful women could not go to the graveside, and blamed Israel for his death.

Back in Munich, her team mates were still competing. Mick won 800 metres gold and Kim just pushed past an East German girl to win the 400 metres silver. They celebrated quietly and wished they were in Tel Aviv to support their friend.

The journey to Israel was too short and painful to leave Rehana with clear memories. She thought a lot about Sam's last moments, thankful that he and Amir had died quickly. Their friends had faced death for eighteen hours. Rehana experienced politeness from those she met, but she did not want to stay in Israel beyond the four days of her visit. There was tremendous hostility towards Palestine that was spilling over into hatred of Muslims. Many felt Sam should not have loved her, and she was afraid there was coldness blowing her way. She wanted to run from the blood of the Middle East, to leave it behind her.

The return flight direct to London passed without turbulence. The El-Al crew kept checking she had what she wanted. She appreciated their concern, but none of it mattered. The open grief she had avoided at the loss of her family nine years ago was made up for now. She did not care if others saw her pain. David had wanted to meet her at Heathrow, but the group of reporters gathered there made it unwise. There would be enough fuss when they saw Peter, who was taking Rehana back to stay in his house. Cameras blinded her as she came through the airport. When Peter got to her, he gripped her hand and led her through the crush.

"Rehana, look this way!"

"Rehana, how are you feeling?"

"Rehana, what did you think of the service?"

They fired their inquisition, desperate for one statement to accompany the fabricated ones already written.

"Would you let her pass!" Peter exploded. "This isn't a freak show."

She was walking slowly but refused to let the press see any tears. In the seclusion of Peter's car she shed a few. The suffering was great: renewed pain at the deaths of her family, and pain at the loss of the man she would have made a new family with. After spending time with David at Peter's home, and asking about their friends, Rehana snatched some sleep. It came easily. In Israel she had barely managed an hour without waking. She got up in the early evening and showered. Peter had cooked and forced her to eat.

Early the next morning, she remembered it was Sunday and felt a need to go home for a while. She took a taxi ride to her flat and looked, emotionless, at the front room. On the day she'd left for Munich - that warm July day when everybody was laughing - she'd left an Olympic souvenir magazine on the sofa. Now she sat down and looked through it. Most of the medal predictions had come true. She remembered her excitement at going to the Games, at running for her country, never dreaming that it would bring with it love. How fast life moved at times. She went to the store to see Daniel and Lita, and around the corner to her Aunt Lakshmi's home. She ran back to Hampstead, attempting to bury her pain in the physical pain of the run. It did no good and when she walked to Peter's front door she was crying. He told her not to feel bad, that she could not expect to feel right for a long time, but she refused to believe him. She urgently needed to shake off Munich and get back to her happier self.

Two days after returning from Israel, she agreed to give a press conference. She was brave to do it, though there really was no choice. Kevin was there, despite his reluctance to take part. Rehana had invited him. She came into the hotel room with Peter at her side. He asked the press to be brief, promising that everyone would get an opportunity to speak. Rehana answered each question slowly. She was taken back to the night before the horror and a wish, however illogical, that she could share this ordeal with Sam. Somebody asked her how she felt about being champion of the world. It sounded so frivolous.

"How far are Black September from achieving their aims?" another asked.

"Their aims are not going to be achieved this way," Rehana said. "Palestine won't come about by killing people. A lot of Palestinians were killed by Israel when it was founded. They won't be brought back by more people dying."

"What's the answer?"

"Negotiation." It was more than Sam and Amir had got. "A shift in the way Israel thinks." She made her statement clearly, with confidence that what she believed was right. "There are no chosen people really, are there? Everyone is equal."

She took Peter's hand and he called a halt. A respectful silence haunted the conference room as the champion rose. Around the world, journalists would begin to write their comments. As Rehana left the hotel she felt something had trapped her spirit. She had no ability to pray. She tried and the words got confused. She forgot her Arabic and was ridden with guilt. Abi had said that he too had lost faith, but how could that have happened when his parents continued to worship? Peter had never seen Rehana in such bad shape. She had always been slight, but strong. Now she was vulnerable. She was not watching her health. He asked her what good it would do if she got ill, and she said it made no difference; that without a family who cared? Peter said that every athletics fan in the country did. "Look at all that mail," he said. "Do you think people write just for nothing?"

Rehana was back in her apartment. Though Sam had never shared her life in Golders Green, she missed him.

What once had been pleasurable - living in a Jewish suburb - suddenly became intolerable. David came to see her each day. After one week, he spoke out. "Rana, how much weight have you lost?" He had not seen her eat for days.

"I don't know. You know I don't weigh myself."

"When are you eating?"

She did not reply, and did not even care when he opened her fridge to find only milk inside.

"Right, get your coat."

"Just leave it, Dave."

"No. This is not going to go on. You've had a terrible time *but you've won the Olympic medal!* For God's sake pull yourself together. You've got to stay strong."

She took her coat and walked to his car. She did not want the meal he made her eat, but he was in warlike mood. The Cypriot waiters in the old Finchley café watched, amused. They had seen the two runners come in since 1966 and had served them breakfast, lunch and tea. Seeing their mirth as David lectured her on the need to eat, Rehana began to laugh.

8

1973 was the year of another handsome Israeli, Uri Geller, who broke forks with his hand. It made it harder for Rehana to keep Israel out of her thoughts, but she was succeeding in getting strong. As time passed, she realised Peter had been right. Her strength of spirit was returning. She ran in the Europa Cup in Edinburgh later that summer, and international contests in Oslo and Dublin. Her prime form had not gone away and she won every race just outside her Commonwealth record time. As the season ended, she flew to Georgia for Neal's wedding, and made her first visit to Pakistan. She had put off going, afraid she had offended her family there by her public love for Sam. She took Kim with her and they stayed in a hotel, visiting the relatives together. No one talked about Sam, nor did they mention marriage, but there was much talk about Islam. In the peace of her grandparents' Karachi home, Rehana was finally able to pray. Perhaps it was the love around her that did it, the tolerance of her family in welcoming her as she was.

In August she returned to Israel for the first anniversary of Sam's death. Abi recited Kaddish at his parents' home and later took Rehana to the beach. She spent time with Abi and Leah, and flew on her final evening to Jerusalem. Looking out over the Red Sea, she felt closer to God. The sky was blue. Munich seemed so long ago, a hazy episode in a violent drama. She was back running but her life stood still in the silence of the Middle East. She prayed for a settlement, but in the sun and silence of that evening she could not have foreseen the fruitlessness of her prayer. Ahead lay many more innocent victims. The future of her world was bloody, and she had a cold feeling when she walked away.

As the year ended she was invited with other top athletes to a lunch with the Prime Minister in anticipation of the January Commonwealth Games. A crowd stood outside when the athletes started to leave. Somebody whispered: "That's Rehana Hassan." A young boy hurried over for an autograph and she knelt down to sign it. She quickly moved on. A reporter chased her and asked her what her plans were for the Christchurch Commonwealth Games. She had decided to drop the 800 metres and concentrate on working for the 1500 metres world record.

Christmas came, and the New Year. She was repeatedly trailed on nights out; each paper wanted an exclusive photograph of a new man in Rehana's life. They were always disappointed, but not when she ran in New Zealand. Once again she took gold, and her speed promised further victory at the European Championships in Rome. But to retain her Olympic title in Canada, as new girls from the Soviet bloc continued to emerge, she had to perfect world record time. David continued to train with her through the next eighteen months. At the end of 1975 he gave up competition athletics to train young people and raise his family. He accepted a deal from ITV in London to provide commentary at Grand Prix events, and teased Rehana with the thought that he would be analysing her performance on national television. He still went running with her. He was sure she would get the world record.

At a pre-Olympic meeting in Rieti, Italy, in late June 1976, Rehana ran the 1500 metres in 4 minutes 2 seconds, 3 seconds over the new Soviet Union world record. She left the track, jubilant, for her hotel room. The English radio service said an Air France jet, carrying 130 Jewish passengers, had been hi-jacked on its way to Israel. Much as she despised the tactic, Rehana knew why the Popular Front for the Liberation of Palestine had done it. As Israel's intransigence mounted, terrorists felt they had no choice.

The hi-jacked plane landed in Idi Amin's Uganda. Although Israeli commandos launched a brilliant raid, three of the hostages died. It brought back horrible memories. TV stations made comparisons between the incident and the Munich killings, never failing to stress that this was an Olympic year. For days afterwards, photographs of Sam and his friends were on the screen. Rehana prepared for the Montreal Olympics in silence.

9

On a humid July morning at Heathrow, Britain's 1976 Olympic track athletes came together for their journey to Quebec. Rehana faced some difficult moments - the Olympic symbol on bags and tracksuits took her back to July 26th, 1972, when the only dream ahead of her was victory at the Games - but other moments brought smiles. Britain's long hot summer had begun, and the runners were heading for a hot summer in Canada too. This time they barely noticed the security checks, and boarded their plane for the trans-Atlantic flight.

As they cruised above the ocean, Rehana stretched back in her seat. "Would you like a paper, Miss Hassan?" a stewardess asked. She was pulled from deep thought and took 'The Guardian', which made her wonder which flight Kevin was on.

"Oh shit," she heard Mick say behind her. "Look at this."

He passed her a paper which said the black African nations were considering a boycott of the Games. Mick was the 800 metres Olympic champion. His foremost rivals were black Africans. "New Zealand's rugby team toured South Africa, and because the IOC won't discipline New Zealand, the Africans want to withdraw," Mick read out. "I don't believe it."

"It might not happen," Rehana said.

"But if it does we're in a Mickey Mouse contest."

Mick was an emotional man. By the time they landed in Montreal he had convinced the entire team that Africa was going to pull out. "It's because of Soweto," he said. "We have to suffer, but apartheid carries on."

Rehana and Kim had made it to the Olympics together again and there were several new additions to their team. Most had been a little scared of the Munich medallists at first. Now they were much more at ease. Rehana and Mick were team captains, and it was not going to be fun if Africa pulled out. A lot of motivation would be needed. Kim unpacked fast and went for a tour of the impressive stadium. Rehana stayed in, planning to unpack slowly and avoid the press outside. What on earth did they want now?

"Rana." She was standing at the window when David came in. "Coming for a walk?"

She shook her head and he knew she was crying.

"What are you looking at?" he asked gently. "It's only buildings through there."

"Security's very tight this time, isn't it? Look at that guard."

"Come on, forget that." David took her hand. "They've just learned a lesson, that's all."

"I thought I was over it."

"You are, but you're at the Olympics again. You're bound to remember."

"Why do the press keep asking how I feel?"

"Oh Rana - it's their job. They always do that. If you don't talk, they print it anyway. Kev Sommerton's okay; talk to him and forget the others. He's been looking for you."

She wiped her eyes. "Okay, you're right. Let's get out."

They walked into the sunshine, hiding from the press. Before long, there was a smile on Rehana's face again. David could always make her feel good. They returned later to the Village, where the only talk was of boycott. Their African friends were shaken. Mick was getting political, telling reporters to lobby the UN. There was a lot of canvassing, and negotiation by the IOC, but by the following day, some of the world's greatest runners and hurdlers left Montreal.

"Is the boycott justified, Rehana?" Canadian press asked her.

"No, I don't think it is." She thought of Uganda, whose brutal dictator had the gall to condemn other states. "Anyone with any decency opposes South Africa," she said, "but look at the countries involved. They're all dictatorships, aren't they? South Africa's got what it deserves by not being invited here. We've lost some fantastic athletes because of politics."

The athletes were tired of it all. There was war everywhere - in Lebanon, Angola and Mozambique - and security wherever they looked. When the opening ceremony of the Games took place no one really enjoyed it. The Union Jack flew alongside the red Maple Leaf of Canada. Rehana looked across the stadium for the green and white flag of Pakistan. Still no flag for Palestine. What were they doing running while across the world people were being shot down?

Mick won his 800 metres race well below the world record. He talked to the press afterwards and blamed the African boycott for his lacklustre win. He was not having a great time. After four years of marriage his wife Jan had left him to live with another man. She was pregnant and kept it no secret. Mick began to think he was losing everything. He missed his three year old son, and knew he would still have his wife if he had not spent day and night training.

By the time her own final came about, Rehana was sure her Soviet rival was on steroids. Tatyana Valueva had set a 1500 metres world record of 3 minutes 59 seconds in June, and Rehana had to fight drugs to break it. Her relationship with the Russian was cool. There was a lot of suspicion in the Village about the Communist bloc and none of the friendly rivalry that Mick and his African friends shared. Rehana had a reputation for her warm and generous spirit. She had never openly turned cold on a rival - not even Ute Brauer who she feared had used drugs at Munich - but she barely exchanged even a greeting with Valueva. She could fight a great athlete, but she could not fight steroids.

"Valueva's a threat, that's all," Peter said. "Don't concentrate on her, just get yourself ready."

He was a good motivator, though it struck him that he had very rarely had to push Rehana to do anything. This was probably their hardest challenge.

Canadian TV showed clips of Rehana's Munich victory and steered the memory away from her grief at the '72 Games to her great achievements that followed. A trying British reporter snatched words with her and she said just what he wanted to hear, that she was running to win. She turned suddenly and caught sight of a ZDF camera focusing on her. It was a definite sign of luck. It made her think right away of the welcome she had got in Bavaria, and the charming ZDF reporter who had wanted to know if she was going to marry Sam. She laughed and suddenly realised she was much more relaxed than she had thought.

The sun burned down in the capital of French Canada. Rehana looked across at David, seated in the ITV commentary box. He waved and signalled a V. Peter was in the background, agitated at the time it was taking for the race to start. David sat back for a few minutes while ITV's track boss listed the line up. He heard the man from New Zealand TV describing Rehana as one of the great women athletes of the decade. Catching David's eye, the broadcaster smiled.

"I bet you're a little bit tense."

"You could say that! Valueva looks ready to kill."

"Don't worry, mate, you've got the Queen in your crowd. It's your victory."

The race began against a light breeze. Rehana executed Peter's plan with incredible skill, and as she came into the home straight, the British crowd was beside itself. She felt herself ease past Valueva and turned her head to see the Russian girl in tears. Spontaneously, she took her rival's hand, though the response she got was limp. She shook her head and knelt on the track in exhaustion as the numbers came up on the board - 3:58:5.

"Hassan has got the world record!" screamed ITV. David, ecstatic, rushed from the box to join Peter as his friend began an incredulous lap of honour towards the erupting British seats. Union Jacks were thrust at her. She fell into Peter's arms and David almost fell on top of her. They were all giddy with joy, and Rehana felt so light-headed she could have flown around the track.

She made it back to the locker room and got grabbed by the rest of the team. TV cameras were ushered out, and she flopped into a seat to think hard about what she had done. When she first really started running she had been running away from pain. The loss of her parents and Sana had brought her Olympic gold. Now the loss of a partner had spurred her to a glorious world record - for what else had she had to live for the last four years? - and sent a message to Fate.

After a shower she closed the door on everyone for a quiet moment with Peter. "Do you remember what I said to you when Sam died?" he asked.

"That one day I would feel better," Rehana replied.

Peter took her hand. "You did feel better, and look what you've done. You've got a world record and two Olympic gold medals. You've fulfilled every dream we ever had." He stood up. "Go and get ready for your medal. I'm very proud of you."

Rehana received her second Olympic gold medal from the Queen. Her heart raced when she lowered her head to accept it and heard the enormous roar from the British supporters. Her world record time was truly magnificent, and everyone knew it was not aided by steroids. "The Queen of British athletics receives her honour from Her Majesty the Queen," enthused ITV. She turned for the playing of the anthem, and had tears in her eyes at the mixed feelings inside her. Commenting back in West Germany, ZDF said, "We can guess what Rehana's thinking about right now. For sure this tremendous victory will give her comfort."

The night flight to London on August 14th was hit by air turbulence. It was the twenty ninth anniversary of the founding of Pakistan, and nearly Rehana's twenty ninth birthday. The athletes were tired and most slept. Rehana was not quite at ease on the plane and tried to read. The seat beside her was vacant and Kevin slipped into it.

"Hi. You look in need of a chat."

She laughed. "I don't always cope too well with flying."

"Even on an official jet? How are you feeling?"

"Okay. Tired."

The turbulence subsided. Kevin unfastened her seatbelt.

"I think you can take it easy now. Can I get an interview?"

She hit him on the arm. "You can't just talk, can you? Okay, but only because it's you."

"Thank you." He pulled out a notepad and grinned. "Miss Hassan, are you going for a third Olympic gold?"

She was amused at the idea. "I think it's time somebody else took over, don't you?"

The plane landed at Heathrow in the early morning. Kevin was still interviewing her as they walked through the baggage hall. "What's your evaluation of the boycott, Rana?"

"New Zealand was wrong, but it was wrong of Africa not to take part."

"What are your plans now?"

"Sleep. Look, you can get a ride back with me, but no interviews!"

10

Joy at seizing the world record so superbly was quickly forgotten in the quagmire that lay ahead. Kevin was in his London office when his editor Ann Bray handed him a copy of 'The Sun'.

"Look at this!" she stormed.

They looked at the sports page headline:

"Black is not British". It said that a British runner had questioned Rehana's eligibility to run for Great Britain.

"Of course, they don't name anyone!" Kevin hissed. "What is this crap?"

"Bob Davies has gone to town on this," Ann said. Bob Davies had been sports editor of 'The Sun' for two Olympic Games. Now he stated his view, that Rehana's victories and world record could not be as great a cause for celebration as those of a white runner would be.

"Miss Hassan carries the Union Jack when she runs," he wrote, "but she is of Asian immigrant parents and is coached by a Dane. She may have the world record, but is it a British one?"

'The Sun' was read by over three million people in Britain, and the feature launched a furious public debate about the acceptance of Asians, Africans and West Indians in 1970s Britain. The racist National Front seized the opportunity to restate its demand for all non-whites to be repatriated, and to Keep British Sport White. Kevin quickly established the source of the story. She was a woman named Deborah Lane, an English counties middle distance champion who had not even made it to the Amateur Athletics Association championships, let alone the Montreal squad. She had not come up to Rehana's most average race times.

Bob Davies had planted the article with cruel intent, knowing it would boost the sale of his paper among what he thought was an increasingly nationalist Britain. He knew that Deborah Lane supported the National Front. Her brother was a National Front local councillor. When Kevin found that out, he told Peter, who said he should go public on it. Politics might not be something Peter wanted Rehana involved in, but this was too insulting to ignore. He was outraged. It was now 1976; since the late 1960s he had seen Rehana pilloried for having a dark skin. Kevin and Ann put a controlled and well-researched article out two days later. They published Deborah Lane's name and slated the use of words such as "immigrant" when Rehana was English-born. In addition, they listed the British sports clubs that had gained from her patronage and fund-raising over the years. It was a valiant effort at answering Davies back, but everyone could see Rehana had taken a knock. It was no easy ride being a British Asian champion.

Kevin ran into Bob Davies at a party thrown by FA Cup winners Southampton the next weekend.

"You racist," he harangued. "Why did you do it?"

"A bit of controversy keeps us all going," Davies shrugged. "No harm done."

"What about all the brown and black kids trying to get into sport? You've done them a lot of good, haven't you?"

"You're an idiot, Sommerton, you know I was right. This isn't Paki-land."

"Pakis*tan*, Davies, it's called Pakistan! Watch it; your lot are on the way out!"

"Hey, what is this? Do you fancy Hassan or what?"

"You make me sick, Davies. Maybe I do!"

He pushed Davies aside and left the hotel for some air. Rehana was a special friend, and of course he 'fancied' her. He had meant to tell her once, long ago, but Sam came along and Kevin suppressed the thought. Now he was married, but those old feelings could not help but be aroused by Bob Davies's remark.

He took Rehana to dinner the next day. The waiters in the Mumtaz Mahal nearly dropped their menus as the champion walked in. Kevin observed that this made her very shy. He admired how she turned a blind eye when they served the wrong starter.

"I had a ruck with Bob Davies yesterday. He accused me of fancying you."

Rehana stopped eating. "What did you say to him?"

"I said that maybe I did."

"Kevin - did you mean it?"

"Yes I did. Sorry, it just came out when he kept on at me." He poured a glass of wine as Rehana sipped cold water. "I couldn't help it. Bob Davies is a racist. His article brought out some feelings in me I didn't know I had." She did not answer and was relieved that he carried on talking. "I'm very happy with Ros. I just wanted to say this to you. Are you uncomfortable?"

"No." Rehana smiled and reached over to touch his hand. "Thank you. You're a good friend."

If Kevin found his emotions mixed by Davies, Mick was in turmoil. His divorce had come through: after two years of bitter public rivalry, and a violent fight for sole custody of their son, Mick and Jan were legally ex-husband and wife. Jan was about to raise her lover's child in the home she and Mick had bought together. It was a mess, and their son Simon was horribly caught up in it. Rehana always took Simon off when he came to running sessions with his dad. He was nearly four years old and was not sure what Mick expected of him. Whenever he saw his parents together he saw only anger. He loved racing with Rehana on the track and she loved having him around. She made Mick realise that he needed to be lighter with his son. He found Simon asleep one afternoon in the locker room as Rehana got ready to go.

"He's been asleep for a while," she said.

Mick hesitated.

"I have to take him back to Jan. Rana, can you come back with me? I hate doing it alone."

"I don't need to see Jan?"

"No. Just please sit in the car. It's the bit afterwards I hate."

They drove slowly and parked behind Jan's car. Rehana watched Mick carry his sleeping son to the front door, and saw Jan come to it. He got back in the car with tears in his eyes, but refused when she offered to drive.

"Mick, come back with me for a bit."

"Okay."

He found it easy to talk when they got to her flat. They seemed to for hours. Rehana took his hand, but then instinctively moved to hold him and could not help kissing him. Though it was sudden, it was no shock to Mick.

"I don't want to hurt you," he said. "Promise me you really want this."

"Come on, Mick, you won't hurt me. I know what I want."

It was just the right moment. Both full of need and desire, and with a friendship stretching back to the days before Munich, they really did not have any doubts.

"What are we going to do?" Mick said.

"I don't know - what do we have to do? We're okay as we are."

"God, Rana, why did I marry Jan when it could have been you?"

"We loved different people," she said. "Mick, that's over. Jan's not your wife. You haven't been unfaithful you know, this is okay."

"Just stay here," Mick murmured.

Rehana laughed. "This is my flat!"

"You were so passionate," he said in the morning. "I felt really loved."

"I don't give it lightly, Mick." Rehana wished she'd had time to with Sam. "We've known each other for a long time."

They had to prepare for a Grand Prix race in Sheffield, and Mick went home to pack. They joined Kim and Paul two hours later for the drive to North England. Minutes after reaching their hotel, Rehana was swept away by an excited local journalist and the friends walked to the bar.

Bob Davies happened to arrive at that same hotel soon after, a coincidence he later rued. He faced ice cold silence for the first time in his life when he walked into the hotel bar. As he sat down with his drink, his press colleagues looked over in contempt and Rehana's team mates stopped talking.

Mick headed straight for him. "What are you doing in here, Davies?"

"I have every right to come into this bar," Davies spluttered.

"Yeah, is that right? Who said?"

Paul intervened. "Why don't you leave Rana alone? She's got two Olympic gold medals for this bloody country!"

Kim looked at him nervously. He was not beyond knocking Davies in the jaw. "Paul, let's get some fresh air," she said. He did not move.

Davies put down his glass. "We all have a right to our opinion in this country, Mr Kerr. It is still *our* country. Calm down, there are enough Pakis in England to stand up for your friend." That was all they needed to hear. Mick went to punch Davies in the jaw but Paul got there first. Davies swore and staggered outside, threatening en route.

"For God's sake, Paul, he'll have you in court!" Kim said hotly. "Did you see those cameras go?"

"I don't care. He's not getting away with that in front of me."

It made headlines in the tabloid press, and both Paul and Mick refused to comment. Davies never pressed charges, but Rehana felt a mixture of discomfort and gratitude. Her friends had stood up for her in the all-white world of a Sheffield bar, but being brown and British was getting harder.

The Grand Prix season was coming to an end and the last event was in Crystal Palace, London. It was still a hot summer. The African athletes were flying in for a chance to avenge Montreal. Rehana drove to the stadium late and rushed past reporters firing questions about Sheffield. Why did every little thing have to make a story? She started a warm up to great cheers, but a sector of the crowd suddenly began to chant Deborah Lane's name.

Everyone on the track was stunned. For the first time in British athletics, racists had come out. Rehana kept her head down and sneaked a glance at Kevin and his photographer Tom Byrne. She walked back inside the tunnel to prepare. This was not a good evening. Valueva was on the track, hungry for revenge, and Rehana had to send the racists away in shame.

Each time Rehana Hassan passed, the racialists yelled out. Her anger rose, and made her fly. She easily set an all-comers' record, brushing past Valueva once again, and did not stop running when she won. TV cameras across Europe followed the Olympic champion as she ran straight over to the racists and shouted abuse back in their faces. Some of the crowd broke into applause, but Rehana was not in generous mood. She refused a lap of honour, and any involvement with the Union Jack, and headed for the tunnel for privacy with her friends.

In the morning faces contorted with hate took front page on 'The Guardian'. Tom Byrne's photographs were sold around the world, bringing some shame to Britain. Outside the Finchley club, Rehana made a one-off statement.

"I'm not prepared to talk about my nationality," she said, "because everyone knows I was born in North London and have never lived anywhere else, but I want you to publish exactly how I feel about Miss Deborah Lane and her followers. Deborah Lane is free to say and believe what she wants, but I plan to take her up on everything she says because I believe it is disgraceful. I am angry that a few comments made by a racist athlete should become the basis for a national debate when I have just put Britain at the top of the world in an Olympic event. I should have run with the Union Jack yesterday, but it's been taken over by some ugly people." She was about to walk away, but stopped. "The future of athletics in England is black and white, and in ten years' time Miss Lane is going to have black British champions all around her."

After the first night with Mick, Rehana was another woman. She wanted to forget every moment of pain and savour only that passion, but something far worse than the Davies slur came about. Through late 1976 Mick and Rehana were thought of as a couple. Though living apart, it was obvious their relationship was at another level. Mick was defensive. Press interest in a pending engagement infuriated him, and he began to wish he had never roughed Davies up in public. He began leaving his flat in the morning to find "Paki-lover" and "White Nigger" sprayed on his car. He and Rehana were catapulted into the pages of the gutter press. The constant talk of marriage irritated them both, but they were much too famous to be ignored. Then, in early 1977, they woke to find Jan Hall on the front page of 'The Sun'. Another

Davies coup. To pay Mick back a hundred times over, the headline declared Jan's belief that his father's affair with "a Pakistani" had made her son's life a misery.

"Mick has to realise that people still don't accept mixed relationships," Jan purred. "If it was just him, I'd say good luck, but I don't think it's fair that Simon has to put up with it too."

Rehana's first reaction was to phone Mick. They both knew Simon's only problem was that Jan had made it a problem for him. They read the paper together, sickened at the smug remarks. They wanted to fight back, but it was tough with a little boy involved.

At that moment Mick knew his son would suffer if he and Rehana married or lived together. Simon would be drawn into unpleasant battles, and Jan would play the race card to stop Mick having his son to stay. But though he and Rehana decided to live apart they found it impossible to stop making love, and even Jan had no say in that. Rehana was mad, and began to feel closer to Pakistan. While apparent democracy still flourished, she wore her Olympic medal on a much publicised holiday in Karachi and let British journalists photograph her wherever she went. She told an Urdu newspaper that her inclination at Crystal Palace was to burn the Union Jack; the National Front had hi-jacked it, and it was nothing more than a symbol of English racism. Returning to Britain, she was not the carefree Rehana of before. Nor was Britain a cheerful place. The streets were full of punk hatred, and racists were a confused bunch.

11

THE 1980s

The world's most famous Muslim athlete opened 1980 with a feeling that her running days were over. Women's athletics was lost to the Soviets and East Europeans. The Moscow Olympic Games were hit by politics before the British squad was even chosen. The Soviet army had occupied Muslim Afghanistan, and some governments did not want their athletes to go. Rehana and her friends debated the subject for weeks. Everyone understood why the British team ended up going. How could athletes sacrifice the four-yearly chance of Olympic glory because of the politics of one state? The Americans were staying behind, and - as in Montreal - the Games were not complete. Though Rehana chose not to run in Moscow, she supported her friends who did. But she made her politics quite clear. "Sometimes what happens in the world is so horrific," she told the press, "that you remember how little an Olympic medal means. The Games should not have been held in Moscow after the strangling of Afghanistan."

She had never been made more conscious of fundamentalist Islam. It was the time of the Iranian Islamic Revolution, and the total subjugation of Muslim women. And Pakistan had an Islamic military ruler. The glory days were ending. By the time of Rehana's last public race in Sheffield, her world record was history and she was losing Mick to another life.

Time had caught up with Mick. He wanted marriage and another child. Racism was getting to him and he made the selfish decision to walk away. He began seeing another woman, an Anglo-Saxon blonde, and was too gutless to tell Rehana himself.

"Mick's White Date" declared 'The Sun' on May 2nd. Rehana was following the reports of London's Iranian Embassy siege when her phone rang.

"It's 'The Daily Mail' here, Miss Hassan. Have you seen this morning's 'Sun'?"

"I don't read it," Rehana replied. She was a little irritated that 'The Mail' had her number.

"Do you know a model called Victoria Channing?"

"No. What is this about?"

"She was seen out with Mick Hall last night. There's a photo you should look at in 'The Sun'."

Rehana hung up and sat down slowly. She was contemplating giving Mick a call, when the phone interrupted her again.

"Rana, are you okay?" It was Kim's anxious voice.

"I don't know. I've just had a call from 'The Mail' telling me to go and get 'The Sun'."

"I've got it. Dave phoned me. I'm coming over."

Kim pushed two reporters aside to get into Rehana's flat. "It doesn't take you long to get on to something, does it?" she said.

"We have a job to do," one of them said.

Kim scoffed and went inside. Rehana turned to the photograph on page six and suddenly wanted to slap Mick across the face.

"Bastard," she said. "He's all over her."

"Phone him up and see what he has to say," Kim urged.

"No. He's been withdrawing from me for months. He's not worth it."

Mick still did not make contact with her, and in a way she was glad. Days later she ran into him at an athletics function. Their friends looked over nervously, but Rehana's performance was not that of a victim.

"Mick - how's Victoria?" she said quite clearly.

Mick met her eyes slowly. "I'm sorry, I should have called," he muttered, aware of the silence around him. "I didn't want to hurt you."

Rehana smiled. "I've got other things to think about, Mick. I go for men with courage. You haven't got that, have you?" She walked away calmly, and Mick knew it was over.

"You're a fool," Paul said. "You know you love her. What's this Victoria got, apart from her bloody figure? I can't believe you're the same man who hates Bob Davies."

"Even if you do love Rana," Kim added, "just stay away from her now. You don't deserve her."

The evening ended and Rehana and Kim left together. "I bet Bob Davies is laughing," Rehana said.

"If he is, who cares? He's just another racist."

"You know, it was just sex," Rehana convinced herself. "It might as well be over. Sam was the only one who mattered."

As the summer came to an end Rehana returned to Israel for a short stay. Abi's son looked much like Sam, though only eight years old, and said he wanted to be a runner. She came home to the start of a career with the Sports Council who wanted to combat steroids in sport.

Rehana's involvement would help to spread the message. She settled into her job with confidence. It was time for her to give something back to the sport, and help shape the runners of tomorrow. She left Golders Green and returned to Finchley, to a new flat five minutes from the old club. There would be a lot of coaching to do. Peter had retired and handed the club over to David, and Rehana loved the thought of working with her friend again.

The 1980s were a bloody time for Middle Eastern terrorism. In September 1982, Israel and the Christian South Lebanon Army entered the Palestinian refugee camps of Muslim West Beirut. The events that followed led to universal outrage, as footage of the massacre of Palestinian civilians was shown across the world. Israel's leaders took a heavy blow. From the Pope to London's Chief Rabbi, the action was loathed. Rehana wrote in the strongest terms to Israel's Prime Minister, warning Mr Begin that this was a signal to the Arab people to continue their terrorist action. She was easily proved right. Islamic extremism escalated as the decade moved on. Western hostages were seized on aeroplanes and on the Beirut streets, and Islam became a faith to be feared.

In 1988 Rehana was forty, still with the youthful features of her running years. Her hair was shorter, her body still fit and athletic. Kevin asked her to accompany him and Ros to the Seoul Olympic Games where, in addition to reporting, he wanted to see at first hand the oppression of South Korea's students. She said yes right away. Flying to Seoul was exciting. Life felt calm. Not altogether happy, for it was hard to be alone, but she gained much from her work. In the Middle East, death was constant, as the youth of Palestine rose in the 'intifada'. Munich had done nothing to change the policy of Israel.

94

12

In early 1989 Islam seized the headlines in the most macabre way as Ayatollah Khomeini, the self-appointed religious leader of Iran, sentenced a writer to death. Reading 'The Satanic Verses', there was little doubt that Salman Rushdie had paid an insult to Islam. But the fatwah that followed was an insult too.

Khomeini, whose followers pounded their heads until they bled, declared that Rushdie should die. Across the Muslim world 'The Satanic Verses' was burned, and Rushdie fled into permanent refuge. Rehana had been angered by the writer's approach, but Khomeini angered her still further. He had corrupted her parents' faith, the faith they had raised her in. Aftar and Zakir's Islam was peaceful and forgiving. It commanded love for God and respect for His prophets. Khomeini, a mere human being, had surely twisted the Holy Qu'ran in demanding the head of another. Something in her made Rehana want to speak out. Islam did not deserve bad press. It was Khomeini who did. She chose her moment. At the end of February, she spoke at a press conference on Rushdie's behalf. Though despising the act, she did not despise the man. "Ayatollah Khomeini is not God," she said, "nor is he God's messenger. He cannot punish or forgive, and he is hurting Islam by believing that he can. Muslims who want the blood of this novelist must leave it to God to decide where punishment is due."

As Britain's most popular Muslim, Rehana had clout, and her words made the front pages in Britain and the Muslim world. Days later she left her flat for a radio interview. The milkman outside, a little late, wished her good morning. Rehana exchanged warm words with Gareth Clarke. He was a Welshman, with as much knowledge of Islam as Rehana's friends had had back in the 1960s. He put the milk bottle down and said she had been remarkably brave.

Neither noticed the motorcycle across the road. Gareth could not say afterwards how many shots were fired. There seemed to be so many.

There was blood and confusion. Passers by raced to the front of the flat, and a shocked neighbour covered Rehana's body. She was riddled with bullets, and was lifted gently on to a stretcher. Insanely, the ambulance drove fast, as though speed might revive her. As the famous body was wheeled through Hampstead Hospital corridors, the drivers looked on in silence. News of the killing spread through the capital. Phones rang in every media office, and the hospital reception prepared for the siege. A nurse went through Rehana's pockets, and the shoulder bag shredded by shots, and quietly placed the bloodstained remains aside.

No one in London missed the news. David's phone kept ringing, and he closed the door on it. His brain functioned but he could not get up and move. He sat in his office refusing to take it in, and only stood up when

Kim got there. They found a taxi to take them to the hospital.

"Can't believe the news, can you?" the cabbie said. "Such a beautiful person."

Dr Ali Ahmed met them and led them away from the press. "It was over in a few seconds," he said. "She would not have been in pain." Distraught, they were unable to believe him. They went to see her in a cold private room and took hold of her hand but she was long gone. They located Peter, who could say nothing. He had lost a daughter.

The hospital was crammed full of press as the world heard of the murder of Rehana Hassan. Reporters clamoured to reach the bedside of the wounded milkman but were swiftly turned away. The Shi'ites were lucky that he had survived. A white British victim would not have been a clever move.

Gareth left hospital with his arm in a sling. He said he would not be working in Finchley again. He was deeply affected by the blood and his proximity to death. He could see Rehana's face as she fell, and her shattered body. There had been no scream or dying words. The press would love to know that their former star athlete had left a final message, but there was no romanticism in real life murder.

"Together At Last" proclaimed 'The Daily Mail' in a last tribute, beside an old impromptu photograph of Rehana and Sam. In 'The Guardian' Kevin wrote his tribute in anger.

"All that I know for sure," he said, "is that the people who killed Rehana are not Muslims." And he went on to say that terrorism would not achieve its aim. It had failed to in Munich in 1972, and it would fail again in 1989.

EPILOGUE

Finchley Athletics Club was modernised, with facilities Rehana and David had never dreamed of in 1966. David stood in the locker room and remembered his first meeting with the girl he had mildly fancied. He smiled at the memory of those embarrassing words, and the laughter he and Rehana had shared afterwards. The sun was shining; he hated that. At least darkness and rain matched the way he felt. He needed Rehana. For half a lifetime they had been brother and sister, and he could not see or touch her.

The press wanted to interview him after ignoring him for thirteen years. Much as they shared the shock at Rehana's murder, they would sell thousands of extra papers by milking dry the story of her death. He spoke to no one. It felt ironic to him that Rehana should lose her life at the hands of Muslims, though he too believed that theirs was not the true Islam. Thirteen years after the Deborah Lane incident, Rehana's murder only lessened the British people's tolerance of the immigrant community and its descendants. Few British Muslims spoke out against the killing, and no one condemned it in Pakistan. Though Pakistan had a moderate woman Prime Minister the forces of religion were still rife.

David walked the Finchley track where he and Rehana had run so many hundreds of times. He remembered what his friend had said before the Moscow Games, when Kevin asked her how athletes could square winning medals with the fact that Afghanistan was dying. She had chosen her words with care:

"I sometimes think back to Munich and Montreal, and I remember that at the time we were running, hundreds of thousands of human lives were being lost or tortured. Maybe we were on the earth to create a bit of joy when all that horror was going on. It's impossible to say. All I could do was say what I believed about it all, and hope that people would hear."

The press had been asking David what he best remembered about her. He remembered too much - holding her when she broke down at Sam's side, euphoric hugs when she took the world record - to ever put it into words. He had been there to support and love her when her world turned dark in Munich. She was not here to give that back to him. He walked slowly to the end of the track and knelt down.

The ground felt quite hot, unusual for a February day. He put his hand out and touched the gravel. It was just a way of feeling close to her. There was nothing else he could do.